ADVENTURE ISLAND

THE MYSTERY
OF THE SECRET ROOM

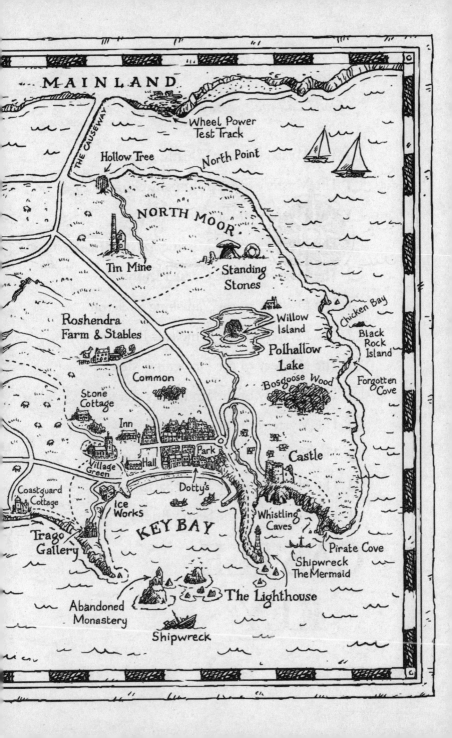

Collect all the Adventure Island *books*

❏ The Mystery of the Whistling Caves

❏ The Mystery of the Midnight Ghost

❏ The Mystery of the Hidden Gold

❏ The Mystery of the Missing Masterpiece

❏ The Mystery of the Cursed Ruby

❏ The Mystery of the Vanishing Skeleton

❏ The Mystery of the Dinosaur Discovery

❏ The Mystery of the Drowning Man

❏ The Mystery of the Smugglers' Wreck

❏ The Mystery of the Invisible Spy

❏ The Mystery of the King's Ransom

❏ The Mystery of the Black Salamander

☑ The Mystery of the Secret Room

THE MYSTERY OF THE SECRET ROOM

Helen Moss

Illustrated by Leo Hartas

Orion
Children's Books

First published in Great Britain in 2013
by Orion Children's Books
a division of the Orion Publishing Group Ltd
Orion House
5 Upper St Martin's Lane
London WC2H 9EA
An Hachette UK company

The Orion Publishing Group's policy is to use papers
that are natural, renewable and recyclable products and made
from wood grown in sustainable forests. The logging and
manufacturing processes are expected to conform to
the environmental regulations of the country of origin.

A catalogue record for this book is
available from the British Library.

Printed in Great Britain by
Clays Ltd, St Ives plc

For Leo Hartas and Roy Knipe,
whose wonderful illustrations and cover art
have brought Adventure Island to life

One

Great Work, Boomerang!

'*Frimbly!*' Scott snorted. 'That's not a real word!'
Jack looked down at the letter tiles he'd arranged
on the board.

He should've known it was a mistake to play Scrabble
with Scott and Emily. His older brother, Scott, hated to
lose at anything – even though he pretended he wasn't
really trying – and their friend Emily had grown up
in the Bed and Breakfast run by her parents so she'd

been playing Scrabble against the guests since she was a baby. Instead of *mummy* or *daddy*, her first word had probably been *quixotic* – with the X on a triple letter score! 'Of course frimbly's a real word!' he said.

'Since when?' Emily demanded.

'Since *forever*!' Jack helped himself to another of Aunt Kate's world-famous double chocolate brownies and flopped back on the sofa. 'It's from Shakespeare, actually.' If Jack had learned one thing from his English lessons at school (and, to be honest, he may *only* have learned one thing) it was that, whatever the question, if you answered with *Shakespeare* you had a fighting chance of being right, or at least sounding a bit brainy. 'Methinks thou art looking a bit frimbly, good sire!' he added, to give an authentic touch.

Scott laughed so much his brownie went down the wrong way. 'What does it mean, then?'

Jack gazed through the window, searching for inspiration. Unfortunately, it wasn't a very inspiring sort of day – which is why they'd ended up playing Scrabble in the first place. They'd already worked their way through Monopoly, Twister and a TV documentary about homing pigeons. Rain was bucketing against the latticed windowpanes, as if Stone Cottage were stuck inside a giant automatic car wash. Jack racked his brains for something that didn't already have a word attached to it. Luckily, making stuff up as he went along was one of his specialities. 'Frimbly?' he said. 'It's that spooky feeling when the hairs go up on the back of your neck.'

Scott threw a cushion at him. 'Yeah, right!' He yawned and stretched. 'I've had enough of Scrabble anyway.' He opened his laptop and went back to hunting zombies on his game of *Total Strategy*.

Emily was fed up with board games too. In fact, she was fed up full stop. It had been raining ever since they'd got back from the Monaco Motor Show a week ago – they'd been V.I.P. guests as a reward for solving the baffling case of a disappearing supercar. After all the sunshine and celebrity, the rain-and-Monopoly combo was a bit of a let-down. Worst of all, Emily thought, how were they *ever* going to find a new investigation to work on in these conditions?

Drift and Boomerang were bored with the rain too. They were lying curled up on the hearthrug. Drift was Emily's beloved Right Hand Dog, a black, tan and white medium-sized medley of many breeds. Boomerang was Aunt Kate's new tabby kitten. Normally, Drift wouldn't be seen dead sharing rug-space with a *cat,* of course, but he made an exception for Boomerang and had called a truce.

Emily watched the rain and sighed deeply, but suddenly she jumped up from the sofa. She'd just remembered that there *was* something more exciting than another game of dominoes to look forward to: Castle Key History Week was starting tomorrow.

Emily couldn't wait! History Week only happened

every three years so she hadn't been old enough to have a proper part in it last time. This year, it was going to be about the Britons – the Celtic people of Cornwall – and their battles against the Saxons who had tried to invade from the East. Everyone on the island would be dressing up and taking part. The grand finale would be a re-enactment of the Battle of Castle Key that took place in 722 AD. 'Have you got your costumes ready for tomorrow?' she asked the boys.

Jack and Scott both groaned – but for different reasons. Jack liked the sound of the battle re-enactment. He was looking forward to charging around pretending to smite things with his choice of lethal weapon. He fancied a massive double-edged sword (he'd even chosen a name for it: the Eliminator) or a mace with brutal-looking spikes, but everything else about History Week sounded far too *educational* for his liking – especially the demonstration of clay pot making for which Emily had signed him up.

Scott, on the other hand, had only one worry, and its name was *tunic*!

The garment that the organizers had given him to wear had clearly been designed for a three-year-old.

It wasn't even long enough to call itself a mini-skirt!

When Scott had tried the hideous item on last night he'd seriously considered running away from Stone Cottage to avoid having to wear it in public. Perhaps he could go and join his dad, who was away on an archaeological dig in the remote jungles of Cambodia – which is why Scott and Jack were staying with Aunt Kate for the summer. But, apart from the dreaded tunic, he loved everything else about staying in Castle Key, so he'd decided against that idea. And anyway, he was fairly sure that the twelve pounds fifty he had left of his birthday money wouldn't get him to Cambodia!

Scott's contemplation of the Tunic Problem was interrupted by Boomerang suddenly leaping ninja-style across the hearth, where she began to scrabble at the base of the stone chimney breast that surrounded the fireplace. Then she crouched, staring at a crack in the stone, ears back, hackles up, stripy rump quivering – like a wild tigress preparing to pounce on an unsuspecting antelope in a jungle clearing.

Emily and Jack had noticed the strange behaviour too. 'What's Boo doing?' Emily laughed.

Jack shrugged. 'Must be a mouse behind there.'

Boomerang flicked out her razor-sharp claws from their velvety pads. Suddenly she flattened her body to the ground and shot through a tiny hole in the stonework.

Scott, Jack, Emily and Drift stared in disbelief.

A muffled mewing sound came from behind the stone.

'Oh, no!' Emily cried. 'She's stuck!'

The three friends tried calling Boomerang's name and

tempting her out with morsels of tuna and a wiggling string. Nothing worked.

'We'll have to try to make this hole bigger somehow,' Scott said.

'What with?' Jack snorted. 'You'd need a sledge-hammer to make a dent in this stuff.'

Scott sighed. Jack was right. The chimney breast had been constructed from slabs of rock so gigantic they must have been leftovers from Stonehenge. He was starting to get seriously worried now. The mewing was getting more feeble. Maybe they should call Aunt Kate from the kitchen – or the fire brigade.

Out of frustration, Scott jabbed at the gap and shoved the stone as hard as he could. To his astonishment, it moved. He pushed again. There was a grinding noise of stone against stone. The whole massive, colossal, ginormous boulder was sliding to one side.

Boomerang shot out with an indignant howl.

'Wow!' Jack breathed. 'How did you do *that*?'

Scott didn't answer. For one thing, he had no idea. And for another, he was too busy staring at the small chamber that had opened up behind the chimney.

'A secret room!' Emily gasped.

'More like a secret broom cupboard,' Jack pointed out. 'It's not very big.'

'What do you expect?' Scott laughed. 'A fitted kitchen and an indoor pool?' He turned back to see Boomerang sitting on the rug washing her ears. 'Great work, Boo!' he said. 'You can join our team as Chief Feline Investigator!'

Boomerang flicked her tail. Cats didn't join *teams*, they worked alone!

Emily ran to fetch her torch from her shoulder bag – she carried a full investigation kit with her at all times – and shone the beam around the little room. But there was nothing to be seen except for a small spider that scurried away into a crack. 'I bet this was a smugglers' hidey-hole,' she murmured. 'They must have stashed their loot here in the olden days.'

'Ooh, or maybe one of the Smuggling Carters hid in here,' Jack breathed, 'to escape from the tax men.'

Jack and Scott had recently discovered that they were descended from a famous family of Cornish smugglers. Jack had been obsessed with old smuggling stories ever since. He stepped inside the little room. 'Slide the stone back across,' he told Scott. 'I want to see how our ancestors felt when they were hiding.'

Scott pushed the heavy stone back into place. 'I'm leaving it open a bit,' he said. 'You might get stuck.' He grinned at Emily. 'Although it *is* tempting!'

'What's it like in there?' Emily shouted.

'Dark!' Jack called back. The voice seemed to come from the solid stone. 'I'm sure I can sense the spirit presence of one of my great-great-grandfathers. And it's dead spooky.'

'Don't you mean *frimbly*?' Scott laughed.

'Exactly!' Jack shouted. 'I told you it was a real word! Close it a bit more. I want to get the full-on smuggler-on-the-run experience!'

Scott pushed the stone until only a crack remained. 'What's the "experience" like now?' he called.

There was no reply.

Scott rolled his eyes. Jack was so predictable! No doubt he thought it would be a hilarious trick to get them all worried and then make them jump out of their skins by springing out when they pulled the stone back. Either that, or he was speechless with terror because the spider had reappeared and run up his shorts.

Scott curled his fingers into the gap and heaved the stone open again.

But Jack didn't leap out at them, because Jack wasn't there!

Two

The Keepers of the Key

Scott, Emily, Drift and Boomerang stood in a row peering into the empty space where Jack had been.

'I'm down here!' came a voice from below.

Emily stepped forwards.

'Look out!' the disembodied voice yelled.

Scott pulled Emily back just in time. Emily shone her torch down at the floor. But there *was* no floor.

'It's a trapdoor,' Scott said, kneeling for a closer look.

Now he could see a flight of rickety wooden steps leading down into a black void.

Scott and Emily felt their way down the stairs, Drift following close behind. They found Jack sitting on the bottom step.

'I felt a sort of bump on the ground,' he explained. 'I just scuffed at it with my foot. Next thing I knew I was scooting down these steps on my bum! Not recommended in shorts,' he groaned. 'Even my splinters have got splinters!'

Jack's voice tailed off as Emily swept her torch beam in a slow arc.

The three friends stared in awed silence.

They had entered a large underground room.

The rough walls were whitewashed. The floor consisted of a few flagstones set into the packed earth. Several wooden benches were gathered round an old wooden table on which were two pewter candlesticks encrusted with rivulets of wax. Another smaller table, draped with heavy gold cloth, stood against the back wall with a faded tapestry hanging above it.

'It looks like a secret meeting room,' Emily whispered. She wasn't sure *why* she was whispering but somehow the hidden room demanded hush.

Scott ran back up the steps and fetched the box of matches from the shelf above the log basket. As he struck a match to light the soft, yellowish candle stubs the bitter tang of sulphur and burning dust cut through the damp, musty air. It took a moment for the ancient wicks to catch but then the flames trembled and danced, throwing long, flickering shadows against the walls.

Scott examined the items on the table. There was a small bone-handled knife and a stick of hard brown wax. A long white quill feather stood in a pewter inkpot. He picked it up. Dry black powder trickled from the nib.

Meanwhile, Jack and Emily had taken the other candlestick and were checking out the other table. Jack tugged the gold cloth and it slithered to the ground. A cloud of dust billowed up, making him sneeze so hard it blew out the candle. By the light of Emily's torch they saw that it wasn't a table after all, but a large chest made of treacle-dark wood, richly carved with crowns and ferocious dragons.

'It's a treasure chest!' Jack whispered. 'It's stuffed with rubies and diamonds and gold bars. Let's open it. What are we waiting for?'

Emily beckoned for Scott to join them and together they pushed up the heavy lid. It rose slowly on creaking hinges.

Drift and Boomerang padded closer as if they, too, were curious to see what lay hidden within the old chest.

Scott held up his candle. Emily shone her torch inside.

Jack groaned in dismay.

Where were the sparkling jewels? Where were the coins, the ingots, the *booty*?

Apart from the dust motes dancing in the torch beam, the chest was empty.

Jack was outraged. What was the point of having a creepy underground room hidden beneath a trapdoor behind a secret stone entrance if you weren't even going to keep any decent treasure down there?

But just then a scroll of paper slipped out from under a frayed leather flap inside the lid and fell into the chest. Emily was so quick to reach in and grab it she pitched into the chest headfirst. Scott and Jack pulled her out by her t-shirt.

Hardly pausing to shake the dust from her hair, Emily held up the scroll. The thick cream-coloured paper was mottled in shades of brown, like a cappuccino sprinkled with chocolate. The edges were curled and tattered. The ribbon that tied it might once have been bright scarlet but was now the colour of dried blood.

'Open it!' Jack hissed. 'It's a treasure map. I know it!'

'Or a priceless historical document,' Scott breathed.

But Emily was sure the scroll contained a message from a spy ring to a secret agent. Almost certainly in code. Slowly, she slipped off the ribbon and unfurled the stiff paper.

They all leaned in closer.

At the top of the page in old-fashioned loopy handwriting were written the words:

Beneath this mysterious heading was a list of names. '*Carter*,' Scott read out. '*Goff* . . .'

'Carter! That's us!' Jack cried. 'I told you this was something to do with the Smuggling Carters.'

Emily peered at the list. The next name looked like Carrow. The following two names were missing, one blotted out by a patch of rusty mould, while the other appeared to have been a three-course meal for a family of beetles. The last name on the list was so faded only the last two letters, 'c' and 'k', were legible.

At the bottom of the scroll were the words *In the Year of Our Lord, 1755.*

'The names are all written in different handwriting,' Scott pointed out. 'It must have been an agreement of some kind.' He pointed to the quill pen and ink. 'Looks like they signed the document at that table.'

'The Keepers of the Key,' Jack mused. 'What's that all about?'

'It's like the nursery rhyme,' Emily said. She chanted in a singsong voice:

'*Keepers of the Key,*
What will you be?
Smuggler, smith, hunter, priest.
Farmer, fisherman, king!'

Scott and Jack stared at their friend. She *looked*

normal enough – well, as normal as she ever did, with her long tangled hair flying out in all directions and her dark eyes shining in the candlelight – so why was she suddenly spouting gobbledygook about hunters and priests and kings?

'What are you on about?' Jack laughed.

'It's a kids' rhyme,' Emily said. 'Everyone knows it. Like *Eenie-meenie-miney-mo*.'

'Oh, *that*!' Scott said as if it were suddenly all making sense. 'Like *Tinker, tailor, soldier, sailor . . .*'

Emily nodded.

Scott shook his head. 'Nope, sorry, never heard of it.'

Jack grinned. 'It must be a Castle Key local speciality. Never made it to London.'

'So what does it mean, Em?' Scott asked.

Emily shrugged. 'No idea! I always thought it was just a nursery rhyme.'

Scott sat down on one of the wooden benches. 'A lot of nursery rhymes are based on real events in history. Like *Ring a Ring o' Roses*.'

Jack laughed. 'What? You mean the famous historical event when people stood round in a circle holding flowers and sneezing so hard they fell over?'

'No, you wombat! It's meant to be about the plague. The ring of roses means a red rash. That was one of the symptoms. And so was sneezing. All fall down means . . .'

Jack held up a hand. 'I get it. Everybody dies.' He

mimed a throat-slitting action. 'How nice! And people say that computer games are gory!'

'*Keepers of the Key* is such a random phrase,' Scott said. 'It can't be a coincidence. That nursery rhyme must have something to do with this scroll, and with whatever happened in this room.'

'I agree,' Emily said slowly as she closed the lid of the chest with a spine-tingling creak. She turned back to the boys. 'So what was this key they were pledging to keep for another year? What door did it open and what was behind it?'

Jack shrugged. 'I don't know, but I have a feeling we're going to try to find out.'

'Well, *maybe* . . .' Emily pretended to be making a difficult decision. Then she laughed as the lid of the chest banged shut. 'Just try stopping us!'

Three

A History Mystery!

The friends blew out the candles, climbed up through the trapdoor and pushed the mighty stone back across the entrance behind them.

Then they all sank down on the sofa. For a moment nobody spoke. The living room – with its flower-patterned curtains, crowded bookshelves and old-style telly in the corner – looked the same as it had before they'd found the secret room. The rain was still rattling on the windowpanes. They could almost have imagined the whole thing, and yet, there was the scroll lying on the coffee table in front of them.

Emily took her notebook from her bag. It was a beautiful new one with a midnight-blue satiny cover and pages edged with silver. She opened the book, inhaled the delicious scent of fresh paper and smoothed down the first page. Then she wrote *OPERATION KEY* and underlined it twice using a silver pen she'd bought specially.

She started by copying out the information from the scroll.

The Keepers of the Key
we renew our pledge for the coming year
Carter
Goff
Carrow
(missing)
(missing)
. . . ck
In the Year of Our Lord, 1755

'We're looking at something that happened over two hundred and fifty years ago,' Scott pointed out. 'The trail might have gone a little cold by now.'

Jack grinned. 'It's a history mystery!' He looked up as he heard the kitchen door open across the hall.

'I wonder if Aunt Kate knows she's got a secret room in the basement.'

Scott laughed. 'I think she might have mentioned it if she did! It's not the kind of thing you forget.'

Jack shrugged. 'I wouldn't bet on it. She *"forgot"* to tell us she used to be an international spy until we found out for ourselves!' He jumped up from the sofa. 'I'll go and ask.' He picked up the empty chocolate brownie plate. 'We could do with a top-up anyway.'

Seconds later, Jack was back from the kitchen without Aunt Kate or the brownie plate but with a piece of rolled-up paper in his hand.

'What's that?' Emily asked. 'Another scroll?'

Jack struck a theatrical pose, unrolled the note and held it at arm's length. He read it out in a deep booming voice, like a town crier. *'I have gone next door for a coffee with Mrs Roberts,'* he proclaimed solemnly. *'Back soon. Aunt Kate. Kiss, kiss.'*

'We could go and talk to Old Bob,' Emily suggested. 'He knows a lot about local history.'

Scott and Jack agreed. Old Bob had run his fishing boat from Castle Key harbour for as long as anyone could remember. He knew all there was to know about the island, had a wise old saying on every subject and a story for every occasion.

Emily checked her watch. 'He should be unloading his boat down at the harbour now. If we're lucky we'll catch him on his way to Dotty's for a cup of tea.'

Before they left Scott ran up to the bedroom and stowed the scroll safely in his bedside drawer. Then he pulled on his waterproof jacket and some wellies he'd borrowed from Aunt Kate's cupboard. They were so old Noah could have worn them while working on his ark but, in fact, they had *Leo Carter* written inside. Leo Carter was Jack and Scott's dad – he and his brother, Tim, used to stay at Stone Cottage when they were boys too. Aunt Kate was actually *their* aunt, which made her Jack and Scott's great-aunt, but nobody had ever worried about that. She was plain Aunt Kate to everyone.

The three friends, along with Drift, of course, splashed their way down Church Lane, across the square and through the narrow streets to the harbour. They soon spotted Old Bob unloading crates of fish from the *Morwenna*. He was covered from head to toe in a dark blue oilskin cape; all that was visible beneath the hood was a pair of bushy white eyebrows and the tip of a weather-beaten nose. As he worked, he exchanged a shouted word or two through the driving rain with the younger man working on the boat at the next mooring. Jack recognized Old Bob's nephew, Ryan Trevithick.

The friends offered to help. To Jack's relief, the two men had almost finished the job already. It wasn't so much that Jack was lazy (although there were several teachers who might disagree with that), but dead fish gave him the collywobbles. Those horrible snaggle-toothed monkfish faces were still making regular appearances in his nightmares since last time he'd helped out at the harbour.

'What can I do for you three, then?' Old Bob asked as they crossed the seafront road and dripped their way into Dotty's Tea Rooms.

'Have you ever heard of the Keepers of the Key?' Emily asked.

Old Bob peeled off his waterproofs. He was wearing his ancient blue jumper, shapeless jeans and a woollen cap underneath. He ordered a mug of tea and took his time stirring in the sugar. He sipped, then leaned back in his chair and sighed contentedly.

Jack wondered whether the old man had forgotten the question and if it would be rude to remind him. But Emily shook her head. You didn't hurry Old Bob!

'That old playground rhyme?' Old Bob asked eventually. *'Keepers of the Key, What will you be?'*

Scott nodded eagerly. 'Do you know what the rhyme is about?'

Old Bob narrowed his eyes as if trying to make out an image in the distance. 'Well, there's a legend . . .'

'I knew it!' Jack said under his breath. With Old Bob there was *always* a legend!

'My old grandfather used to say that a thousand years ago a secret society was formed here on the island. It was charged with the safekeeping of an object of great importance . . .'

Ryan Trevithick stirred his coffee. 'I remember you telling me that story when I was a youngster, Uncle Bob.' He winked at Jack. 'One of the many!'

'What object?' Emily asked.

'Well, that's just the thing. No one can remember what it was, or who the Keepers were for that matter. The knowledge was lost long, long before even my old grandfather's time. Of course, some did say it was to do with King Arthur.' Old Bob looked up from his tea and wheezed with laughter. 'But people say that *anything* that happened in the old days in Cornwall was something to do with King Arthur! He must have been a very busy man.'

With that, Old Bob took a smartphone from his pocket and began tapping away. 'Now, I'd better get on with checking the market prices for that mackerel.'

Ryan grinned. 'Checking the odds on the horses running at Exeter this afternoon, more like!'

The friends thanked the two fishermen and left the café, bowing their heads against the rain that pounded the seafront.

Emily stopped and gazed out across the harbour, deep in thought. Everything was so grey and waterlogged it was impossible to tell where the sky stopped and the sea began. Old Bob and Ryan's boats bobbed side by side. The traditional dark-green fishing boat, *Morwenna*, and her smarter, sleeker neighbour, *Island Mist*, reminded her of one of those before-and-after beauty makeover adverts in a magazine.

That's when she noticed the faded pattern – like part of a Celtic knot design – traced in cracked yellow paint on the bow of the *Morwenna*, just beneath the name. Emily knew she must have seen it a hundred times but she'd never given it a thought before. She glanced across to *Island Mist*. There was the same pattern! This time it was picked out in stylish dark red on the gleaming white bow.

Emily ran into the café. Old Bob and Ryan were putting their coats back on. 'That pattern you have on your boats . . .' she began.

Old Bob nodded. 'What about it?'

'What does it mean?'

'It's just a lucky charm,' Old Bob said. 'It's something that we've always painted on the boats in our family. My dad did and his dad, and his father before him, no doubt.'

'Fishermen are a superstitious lot,' Ryan added. 'You know, like they say it's unlucky to wear green at sea or utter the word *rabbits*. Why did you want to know?'

Emily smiled and backed out of the door. 'Oh, just curious!'

But there was more to it than curiosity, of course.

Emily had seen that very same Celtic knot pattern woven into the tapestry in the secret room.

Four

The Hunt Begins

As they squelched back up Church Lane, Emily told the boys about the pattern on the two fishing boats. 'I took a photo with my phone,' she said. 'I'm sure it matches one of the patterns on the tapestry in the secret room. Let's check as soon as we get back.'

But as they were setting out their waterproofs and wellies to dry in the kitchen and drying Drift's fur with an old towel, Aunt Kate came in from her visit next door. Although she'd taken a huge golf umbrella, the rain had made her white hair frizz like candyfloss and her glasses fog over. The friends quickly told her about their incredible discovery.

It took a lot to flabbergast Aunt Kate. Scott, Jack and Emily knew that from first-hand experience. They'd presented her with some serious surprises in the course of their investigations – a pair of homeless Dobermans, a runaway prince and an undercover spy to name but a few – and she'd taken them all in her stride. But she looked flabbergasted now!

'A secret room behind the fireplace?' she repeated. 'I had no idea. I think you'd better show me.'

Scott heaved back the chimney stone and opened the trapdoor to reveal the concealed room. Aunt Kate climbed down the old wooden stairs and looked around in amazement. 'Goodness me!' she murmured. 'I'm sure there's no mention of this in the deeds . . .'

'Deeds?' Jack asked, as they climbed back up the steps. 'What are those?'

'They're the legal documents you get when you buy a house,' Aunt Kate explained. 'They tell you who has bought and sold the house before, how much land comes with it and so on . . .'

Scott exchanged excited glances with Jack and Emily. They were all thinking the same thing. If the deeds recorded who owned Stone Cottage in 1755 they could provide a massive clue in unlocking the mystery of the Keepers of the Key.

'How old are the earliest deeds?' Scott asked.

'They start from about 1600,' Aunt Kate said. 'The cottage is even older but the earlier records have been lost . . .'

'Can we look at them?' Jack asked.

'I don't see why not.' Aunt Kate went into the hall and reached down an old wooden box from the bookcase. She blew dust from the top, set the box down on the coffee table and flipped open a gold catch. 'I bought Stone Cottage almost forty years ago,' she explained. 'I was travelling a lot in those days and I wanted a base to come home to in between jobs. I grew up not far away, near Carrickstowe, and I'd always loved Castle Key . . . I knew I'd be happy here.' She smiled at the memory. 'The cottage belonged to an elderly couple before me. They were friends of my parents, in fact . . .'

Luckily, just when it seemed Aunt Kate was going to take them on a guided tour down Memory Lane, a timer beeped in the kitchen. 'I'll leave you to it,' she said, rushing off to take a blackberry crumble out of the oven.

Scott lifted bundles of documents out of the box. As he delved deeper through the layers of history, the paper became thicker and more yellowed, and the text changed from computer-generated to typewritten to hand-scribed. All the papers were embellished with swirling signatures, official stamps and blobs of sealing wax, and accompanied by maps shaded in faded pink and beige.

Jack began pulling out pages at random.

Emily slapped his wrist. 'Stop mixing them all up! I'm trying to arrange them in chronological order.' Starting with the most recent document, which covered the sale of Stone Cottage to Miss Katherine Trelawney (a.k.a. Aunt Kate) in 1972, she set the deeds out in a row along the floor, stretching back to 1602.

The friends gazed down at the three-hundred-and-seventy-year timeline. Amongst the important-sounding legal words like *heretofore* and *notwithstanding* and the snippets of Latin, one thing jumped off the old pages straightaway: every single deed bore the name *Goff*. It seemed Stone Cottage had been passed down through the generations of one family – right up until Aunt Kate bought it.

'Goff!' Jack cried. 'That's one of the names on the scroll!'

Emily picked up the document that covered 1755 – the year on the scroll. '*Thomas James Goff,*' she read out. 'He took ownership of Stone Cottage in 1749.' She examined the next document in the row. 'That's sad. It looks like he died a few years later. In November 1755 the property passed to his wife.'

Suddenly Scott jumped to his feet and ran upstairs. Moments later he was back with the scroll. He unfurled it and placed it next to the old deed. 'Look, Thomas

James Goff's signature on the deed exactly matches the word *Goff* on the scroll. That proves that he was a Keeper. He signed this document!'

There was a solemn hush as they gazed down at the matching signatures. Jack broke the silence. 'But who's this Smithy person they keep going on about?'

'Smithy?' Scott laughed. 'That sounds a bit matey for a set of legal documents. It's like saying Jonesy or Gazzer or something!'

But Jack held up a bunch of papers. 'Look! It says *Stone Cottage, Smithy*, here. It keeps popping up all over the place.'

Scott took the papers and studied them for a moment. 'Oh, I get it! Smithy isn't someone's name,' he explained, 'it's the old word for a blacksmith's place. It looks like the Goffs were the Castle Key village blacksmiths.'

Emily looked up from writing in her notebook. 'No wonder the fireplace in here is so big. It must have been part of the forge where they heated the metal.'

All of a sudden Jack opened his eyes wide and held up his hands. He looked back and forth from Emily to Scott, opening and closing his mouth. Either he was performing a mime of a gobsmacked goldfish or he was having one of his brainwaves! 'We're looking for a key, right?' he said. 'And old Goffy was a blacksmith. I bet he *made* the special key right here in his forge!'

Emily nodded slowly. 'Genius! Of course! A great, big iron key.'

Scott shrugged. He had to admit it was a good idea but he didn't like to give his brother too much credit. 'Or he could have made *six* keys, one for each of the Keepers on the scroll,' he suggested.

'Ooh, yes,' Emily said, suddenly remembering something from one of their previous investigations last summer. 'It could be like that special cabinet the Romaldi family stored the cursed ruby in. Three people each had to put their keys in the lock at the same time to open it.' She looked at the boys with shining eyes.

'What if the key – or keys – are still right here in Stone Cottage?'

The friends searched from the attics down to the secret room in the basement. They moved furniture, prised up loose floorboards, poked at cracks in the plasterwork and felt along the tops of beams.

They found a lot of things: the little silver dog, missing from the Monopoly set since anyone could remember, Aunt Kate's spare glasses, four pounds and twenty-three pence in loose change, five odd socks, seven dead spiders and a Werther's Original toffee (which Jack ate in the interests of scientific investigation!).

But they didn't find a key.

Drift and Boomerang joined the hunt. They had no idea what they were looking for, of course, but Boo proudly presented Scott with a particularly fine mouse skeleton she'd been keeping behind the hall skirting board, and Drift offered Emily a half-chewed tennis ball that he found in the porch.

There was great excitement when Scott found a small iron key between the floorboards on the landing, but it turned out to be a false alarm. It was just a spare key for the old wooden toy box in his and Jack's attic bedroom.

At last they had to admit defeat.

If Thomas Goff had fashioned the secret key in his forge, it was no longer in Stone Cottage.

'Now what?' Jack grumbled. 'We've hit a dead end!'

'Not necessarily,' Emily said, reaching into her bag for her phone and clicking on the photo of the pattern on the two fishing boats. 'We've got another lead to follow.'

Five

Putting the Pieces Together

Scott, Jack and Emily pushed back the stone and descended to the secret room once more. This time they took an antique oil lamp they'd borrowed from the dresser in the kitchen, and hung it from a hook on the wall near the tapestry.

The tapestry was the size of a large bath towel. In the middle, a dragon and a lion were shown fighting in front of a castle tower, all woven in faded hues of rust and beige and blue-green. It was an impressive scene, but the friends were more interested in what surrounded it: an intricate Celtic knot pattern, picked out in green and gold thread, snaking its way around the entire border.

Emily held her phone with the image of the pattern from the fishing boats up next to the tapestry. She tipped her head to one side and then the other. She'd been so sure the patterns would match, and yet, it seemed they weren't the same at all.

Scott took the phone and rotated it a few times. 'There!' he said, pointing to the top left corner of the border. 'If you turn it upside down it matches that little section.'

Emily looked closer. 'Yes!' she murmured. 'I knew it would!' Her eyes glowed with excitement. 'This pattern is all part of the secret.'

'How do you figure that out?' Scott asked.

'It's obvious!' Emily said. 'One of Old Bob's ancestors must have been a Keeper. His surname is Trevithick. The last missing name on the scroll looked as if it ended in *ck*. I bet it said *Trevithick*. Why else would his family still paint part of this pattern on their boats?'

But Scott wasn't sure. 'It's probably just chance. You see Celtic knot patterns like this everywhere. People have them on tattoos and jewellery and all sorts.'

Emily glared at him. 'So you're saying there are people walking around with random tattoos that just *happen* to be exactly the same as this?' She jabbed her finger at the tapestry.

Scott nodded. 'Quite possibly!'

'No way!' Emily snapped.

'Suit yourself!' Scott said. 'You're just seeing what you want to see because it fits your theory!'

Emily was so irate she actually stamped her foot. 'Am not!'

Jack sat on a bench and put his feet up. This was primetime entertainment! Emily and Scott hardly ever argued. Jack and Scott usually did more than enough of that to go round! What were brothers for, after all, if not for practising your confrontational skills? And Emily and Jack often clashed because they both had stubborn streaks a mile wide. Scott was usually the peacemaker. But right now it looked as if Scott and Emily were going to come to blows. And over a stupid old pattern, of all things!

Jack was trying to decide whether to take sides and stir things up even more, when a memory popped into his head. He made his way back up the steps to the living room. When he returned a few minutes later, Emily and Scott were still eyeball to eyeball in front of the tapestry.

'Ceasefire!' Jack yelled.

Emily and Scott whipped round to face him, their angry faces like a pair of gargoyles in the lamplight. 'What?' they snapped in unison.

43

Jack strode across to the tapestry and held up a large piece of drawing paper.

'What's that?' Scott demanded.

'It's a rubbing,' Jack said casually. 'I did it with a wax crayon.'

'I can see it's a rubbing,' Scott said. 'What's it of?'

Emily took the paper from Jack's hand and examined it closely. 'It's another piece of Celtic knot pattern. Where did you find this?'

'On the fireplace in the living room,' Jack said. 'I noticed it yesterday. It's carved into the stone on the hearth. I just remembered when you two started ranting on about those patterns.'

Scott narrowed his eyes suspiciously. Was this one of Jack's pranks to wind him up? 'Oh yeah? How come we've never seen it before?'

'It's usually hidden under the log basket,' Jack explained, 'but I moved it yesterday when we were looking for the key.'

While the boys talked, Emily was rotating the paper and sliding it around the edge of the tapestry. Suddenly she grabbed Scott's arm. 'There! Another match! *Now* do you think it's a coincidence?'

Scott looked. It was true. Jack's pattern matched another segment of the border, this time in the bottom corner. 'Might just be a fluke!' he said gruffly. But he was starting to doubt himself now . . . *Two* chance matches did seem a bit unlikely.

Emily was still staring at the tapestry. 'Old Bob's family have one little piece of this pattern painted on their boats,' she said slowly. 'The Goff family engraved another section on the hearth here at Stone Cottage. I think the patterns are important. They're like pieces of a puzzle ...'

'You mean like a jigsaw?' Jack suggested. 'And the six Keepers on the scroll have one piece of it each.'

Emily nodded.

Suddenly, Scott was so excited he forgot all about his bust-up with Emily. 'Of course! That's why we couldn't find the key yesterday. It's not an actual key made of metal. It's what you get when you fit all the pieces of the puzzle together in the right way. The patterns fit together to make the key that unlocks the . . . well, whatever the Keepers were guarding!'

—

Later, as Emily and Drift were leaving to go home to The Lighthouse for dinner, Emily turned to the boys with a serious expression. 'We'd better not breathe a word of all this to anyone. We're obviously dealing with something really important that the Keepers went to a lot of trouble to keep secret. It might be dangerous if our information falls into the wrong hands.'

As he closed the front door Scott rolled his eyes at Jack. 'Emily seems to think we're living in some sort of spy movie! Like there are enemy forces at work out there who will stop at nothing to uncover our vital intelligence.'

Jack laughed. 'And anyway, how can we give away the secret when we don't even know what the secret *is*?'

'Or how to find it!' Scott added.

Just then the doorbell rang. Emily was back. 'I'll meet you on the high street at ten tomorrow!' she said. 'First day of History Week. Don't forget to wear your costumes!'

—

Sitting up in bed that night, Jack could barely concentrate on reading his *Asterix* comic books. His thoughts kept drifting back to the secret room. 'I bet a million pounds it's something to do with King Arthur,' he told Scott, who was sitting on his bed strumming his guitar.

Scott grunted. He obviously wasn't listening, but Jack didn't let that bother him. 'Those Keeper guys were probably guarding the location of the Holy Grail or something. Like in that Indiana Jones film.' He paused for a moment. 'What is a Holy Grail anyway?'

'It's a special cup,' Scott murmured without looking up. 'It's meant to give eternal life or bring King Arthur back from the dead or something.'

'Yeah,' Jack said. 'I'm sure that's it! Castle Key isn't that far from Tintagel and that's where Arthur lived.' He jumped up, scattering books to the floor. 'Or maybe it's Arthur's sword, Excalibur?' Jack leaped between the beds doing wild swashbuckling moves, complete with air-swishing sound effects. Suddenly he had an even more awesome thought. 'What if one of Old Thomas Goff's ancestors *made* Excalibur in the first place – right here in the forge at Stone Cottage – and that's why his family got the job of guarding its secret location after Arthur died?' He stood in the middle of the room, hands on hips, convinced his brilliant theory was right. 'And our Carter ancestors were in on the secret too,' he added. 'We're on that list on the scroll as well, remember.' He did a backwards dive onto his bed. 'Wow! I can't believe it. This means we're practically Knights of the Round Table!'

Scott couldn't ignore Jack any longer. He looked up and laughed. 'Didn't you hear what Old Bob said? People think that *anything* that happens in Cornwall is to do with King Arthur. Newsflash! It's not!'

Even so, as he put his guitar back in its case, Scott couldn't help wondering if there might just be the tiniest grain of truth in Jack's deranged ramblings. He fetched his laptop and, without letting Jack see what he was doing, searched the internet for any mention of a connection between the Keepers of the Key and King Arthur. As he expected, there was nothing.

He was about to switch off the computer when he noticed a website about research into Arthurian legends. There was a discussion forum on the home page. Maybe it would be worth just asking if any of the experts knew anything about it? Remembering Emily's dire warning about secrecy, he made sure he didn't give any information away.

I'm interested in a society called the Keepers of the Key on Castle Key island, Cornwall, he typed. *Anyone know anything about it?*

The website prompted him for a username.

Scott knew better than to give his real name, of course. He glanced across at Jack who was still rabbiting on about being a Knight of the Round Table. That gave him an idea. *Mad Jack*, he typed into the username box.

But as he turned off the light and closed his eyes there was only one thought running through Scott's head.

Was there *any* way he could get out of wearing that tunic tomorrow?

Going into Battle

Scott's day started well.

He was greeted at the breakfast table by bacon and eggs and a pair of baggy trousers.

'Mrs Loveday dropped these round for you earlier,' Aunt Kate explained. 'They were meant to be part of your costume but they got left behind somehow.'

Scott gazed at the shapeless red and yellow tartan trousers as if they were the coolest item of clothing he'd ever clapped eyes on. He couldn't have been happier if Aunt Kate had presented him with the new season Chelsea strip signed by all the members of the team including Fernando Torres!

After breakfast, Scott and Jack changed into their Cornish Briton outfits – loosely belted tunics, trousers, cloaks and soft leather boots – and set off on their bikes for the high street. The rain had stopped although dense grey cloud still loomed in the west.

They soon spotted Emily cycling towards them, with Drift sitting up in his special basket on the back of her bike. Her long green dress and brown and orange tartan cloak flapped around her. With her chestnut curls tumbling over her shoulders, and her feet bare as usual, she could have stepped straight out of a time machine from the eighth century (apart from the bike, of course!). She swerved to a halt and jumped down, all the while grumbling about her skirts getting caught in the pedals – although Scott could tell she was really quite proud of her ancient Cornish outfit.

The friends locked their bikes outside the mini-market and continued on foot to the common, which was the main venue for the History Week events. 'Wow!' Jack breathed as they looked over the scene. 'It's like something out of a movie!'

It was indeed an impressive sight. The southern end of the common had been transformed into a Saxon settlement, with thatched huts clustered around a large wooden hall. The Britons' camp was to the north, and consisted of colourful tents as well as round reed-thatched dwellings. Crowds of people thronged the two camps and the area in between, all dressed in long dresses or tunics and cloaks. There were stalls and games and demonstrations and entertainers. Small groups of animals, on loan from Roshendra Farm, roamed free. Sheep grazed, goats chased small children and stole food, and a litter of ginger and black piglets raced around, while their mothers snuffled under the chestnut trees. The air was rich with smells of woodsmoke, roasting meat, and damp, muddy grass.

The friends wandered around enjoying it all, watching tug-of-war and archery competitions, playing hoopla and apple-bobbing and listening to Saxon storytellers and Cornish bards. Everywhere they went they spotted people they knew. Aunt Kate was reciting old Cornish poems. Emily's mum was in charge of the spinning and weaving demonstration, while her dad was playing the lute in another tent. Colin Warnock, the curate from St Michael's church, had shaved off his purple Mohican and was dressed as a monk, while Dotty from the café was baking bread on one of the food stalls.

After a delicious lunch – meat from a whole hog roasting on a spit over an open fire, followed by honey cake and washed down with apple juice – the friends split up as they each had jobs to do. Scott was helping to herd the animals into pens while Emily was demonstrating hand-spinning with her mum, teasing out the fluffy sheep's wool and winding the yarn onto a spindle. Jack's job description was *preparing clay for the pottery-making demonstration*.

How hard can it be? Jack thought. *Open the box, take out a lump of clay and pass it to the guy at the potter's wheel.* Unfortunately, eighth-century clay didn't come in a box. *Preparing* turned out to mean bashing a lump of rock-hard mud with a stick, treading it with his bare feet and picking out the stones. It was hard work! When a gong sounded to signal that the first battle re-enactment was about to start, Jack couldn't get away fast enough!

The main battle would be held on the final day of History Week in the grounds of Key Castle. Today's event – which was taking place in a large arena in the middle of the common – was more of a warm-up skirmish.

Jack joined Scott and all the other warriors in the mustering station for the Cornish Britons' army. Meanwhile, the Saxons were gathering on the other side of the common.

The Cornish army was given its instructions by the king, a burly red-bearded fisherman called Jago Merrick. He was ably assisted by his wise advisor, Caradoc, played by Old Bob. Merrick explained that the actual fighting would all be done by members of the Historical Society, who had been practising for months.

The rest of the participants, including Jack and Scott, were more like football supporters or cheerleaders: when given the signal, they were to surge forwards or retreat, scream battle cries or chant in victory.

At last the warriors had their faces daubed with blue woad warpaint and the weapons were handed out.

Jack grinned as he gripped his battle-axe. OK, it was a replica and it wasn't even sharp, and he'd *really* wanted a sword, but it looked pretty realistic. He gave it a little swing around to try it out.

'You may brandish the weapons and rattle them on your shields,' one of the organizers shouted, with a stern look at Jack, 'but you must not hit anyone with them. Irresponsible use of weapons will lead to warriors being asked to leave the battlefield immediately!'

Although he knew it wasn't for real, Jack could feel his stomach churning with pre-battle nerves as he trooped out with Scott and all the other Cornish warriors to line up behind their king and knights. There were cheers from the crowds of spectators. Horns trumpeted. Banners fluttered. Jack's heart hammered in his chest.

From the entrance of the spinning and weaving tent, Emily stood and watched. Women and girls weren't allowed to take part in the battles. She threw down her spindle in frustration. 'It's so unfair!' she muttered to Drift, who was curled up on a pile of unspun fleeces. 'Haven't these people ever heard of Boudicca?'

There was a last-minute delay, as the Saxons, led

by Egbert (alias the Mayor of Carrickstowe) objected to some of the Cornish Britons having changed their leather boots for wellies due to the mud. But eventually the footwear issue was resolved and battle commenced.

Soon Jack and Scott were swept up in the frenzy of war.

'I feel like we're in a scene from *Braveheart*!' Scott laughed as they charged, yelling bloodcurdling battle cries.

Jack was having a great time. Along with the screaming and howling, he threw in a few foot-stomping and tongue-waggling moves that he'd seen the New Zealand rugby players do in their *haka* before matches. It would have been even better if a skinny little guy didn't keep shoving him in the back. Eventually he turned round to protest. 'Watch what you're doing with that shield, mate!'

Jack did a double take! He knew those big brown eyes. And no wonder the guy's scruffy felt cap was bulging; it was stuffed full of long curly hair. And now there was a dog who looked just like Drift running up to join them too. 'Emil . . .' he cried.

'Shh!' Emily hissed, glancing over her shoulder.

'What are you doing here?' Jack whispered. 'I thought girls weren't allowed!'

Emily screwed up her face. 'Have you ever *tried* spinning?' she asked. 'No wonder Sleeping Beauty fell asleep for a hundred years!'

'But where did you get the outfit?'

'I found a spare pair of leggings in the supplies tent. I've just stuffed my dress into them. I borrowed the shield and sword from a boy who's sitting out with a sprained ankle! Come on, we're meant to be doing a war cry. Aieeeeeeeeeee!' she screamed in his ear.

Jack had to admit Emily was far scarier than most of the boys he knew!

All too soon, the blare of a horn signalled that the battle was over.

Dead and injured warriors lay strewn across the common.

Of course, they were only acting. Once the applause had died down, they got up and walked off the battlefield, spattered from head to foot in mud and fake blood, some carrying artificial severed arms and legs, all chatting about how the battle had gone and making plans for the evening.

All except one.

A lone warrior remained lying face down on the battlefield.

'Looks like someone's been hurt,' Scott said.

Emily knew she should slip away quickly and change back into her girl clothes before she was found out, but she couldn't resist going to see what was happening. Along with Scott and Jack and Drift, she ran to join the small crowd that had already gathered round the casualty.

The man's blue and green tartan cloak was spread out around him. Blood oozed from under the back of his helmet, trickling down his neck and dripping into a puddle, staining the churned-up mud deep red.

Jago Merrick, King of the Cornish Britons, reached down and gently turned him over.

Emily gasped and grabbed Scott's arm.

It was Old Bob.

Seven

Family Heirlooms

Emily dropped to her knees and began to clear the mud from the old fisherman's mouth and nose. To her relief, she felt a whisper of breath on her hand.

'Someone call an ambulance!' Scott shouted.

Everyone looked at each other. Nobody had a phone. Mobile phones had been banned from the battlefield in case they went off in the middle of the fighting.

Drift was nudging Old Bob's arm and Jack was trying

to find a pulse when two volunteers came rushing over from the St John ambulance parked out of view behind the stand of chestnut trees. They carefully removed Old Bob's helmet and examined the wound. 'He's had a nasty blow to the back of his head,' one of the first-aiders said. 'Lucky he was wearing a helmet.'

Jago Merrick shook his head in anger. 'One of those bloomin' Saxons must have got carried away with his battle-axe. Typical! They always take it too seriously!'

Old Bob's eyes flickered. His weather-reddened face had turned a sickly shade of greenish-grey. 'I need to tell them . . . he who would be king . . .'

Someone in the crowd laughed nervously. 'All this history's gone to his head. He thinks he's King Arthur or something.'

'It's the concussion, that's all,' the first-aider said, helping his colleague to lift Old Bob onto a stretcher. 'He's delirious. It's alright, mate! Don't try to talk. We'll soon have you in hospital.'

But Old Bob sat bolt upright on the stretcher and pointed a finger at something only he could see. 'Beware the hooded man!'

A shiver ran up Emily's spine. She knew it was just the concussion making Old Bob ramble, but she couldn't help feeling he was looking straight at her as he spoke.

Emily slept late the following morning. From the rattling on the porthole windows of her little circular bedroom on the eighth floor of The Lighthouse, she could tell the rain had crept back again during the night.

As she padded down the spiral stairs to the kitchen on the first floor, she wondered how Old Bob was getting on. As soon as she'd put a piece of bread in the toaster she planned to phone the hospital and find out.

But it turned out she didn't need to. Her mum was in the kitchen loading the dishwasher, talking into the phone tucked under her chin. Or rather, the person on the other end of the line was talking. Her mum was just nodding and saying, 'Uh-huh' every now and then.

'Old Bob's doing fine,' Mum said, looking up and smiling at Emily when the call was finally over. 'That was Mrs Loveday. She's been over to the hospital in Carrickstowe for an update already this morning. They're going to keep him in for a few days' rest. It seems he can't remember how it happened.'

Emily grinned. Who needed newspapers or TV when Mrs Loveday – the Gossip Queen of Castle Key – was broadcasting up-to-the-minute bulletins? The good news was a relief. But suddenly she had a worrying thought. 'Does this mean they're going to cancel the rest of History Week?'

'Oh, no, I don't think so,' Mum said. 'It was just an unfortunate accident.' She closed the dishwasher and glanced at the clock on the wall. 'I'd better go and get ready. Are you coming to help with the spinning display again?'

Emily didn't say a word, but she made a face that suggested she'd rather stick her head down the toilet.

Mum laughed and made a face back. 'OK. Why don't you have the morning off and just come for an hour or so this afternoon?'

Emily hugged her. It wasn't just that spinning was her idea of Death by Boredom, there was also work to be done on Operation Key.

And she'd woken up with a brilliant idea . . .

Emily threw on her waterproof jacket, lifted Drift into his special basket on the back of her bike and pedalled through the rain to Stone Cottage. She found Scott and Jack lounging around the living room, still in their dressing-gowns.

'You slobs!' Emily muttered, as she cleared a pile of bubble-gum wrappers, biscuit crumbs and the latest copy of *Motor Mania* magazine from the sofa and sat down. She gave the boys the news about Old Bob, then pulled out her notebook and briefed them about her idea.

'I kept thinking about that nursery rhyme last night,' she began. '*Keepers of the Key, What will you be?*'

Jack laughed. 'All that *fisherman, fireman, beggarman, thief* mumbo-jumbo, you mean?'

Emily shook her head. 'That's not how it goes. It's *smuggler, smith, hunter, priest. Farmer, fisherman, king!*'

Jack grinned and held up his hands. 'Whatever! But it still doesn't make any sense.'

'Aha! That's where you're wrong,' Emily said. 'In the middle of the night I suddenly realized why I couldn't get the rhyme out of my head. The job titles all line up with the names on the scroll.'

'How do you mean?' Scott asked, one eye still on the game of *Total Strategy* on his laptop.

Emily held out her notebook to show him the list. 'The first name is Carter. We know the Carter family were smugglers, of course.'

'Yeah, Jack *has* mentioned that once or twice!' Scott said with a grin.

'The next name is Goff. The Goffs were blacksmiths.'

Scott was getting interested now. He quit his game without even finishing the level. 'Yeah, that's right,' he said. 'Smith is short for blacksmith!' He took another look at the list. 'The next name on the scroll is Carrow. That means the Carrows must have been hunters.'

Emily nodded. 'And, according to the rhyme, the next two names – the ones we can't read – would be a priest and a farmer. And then a fisherman. We already thought that the name ending in *ck* on the scroll might be Old Bob's family because of the pattern on the boats. And the Trevithicks *are* fishermen. It all fits perfectly!'

Scott thought for a moment. 'Maybe the rhyme

started out as a way of remembering who all the Keepers were without actually giving away their names.'

'That's what I was thinking,' Emily agreed.

But Jack wasn't so convinced. 'What about the king?' he asked. Or rather, because he'd just popped a giant gobstopper into his mouth, it came out as 'Ock a wowk a kig?' He removed the gobstopper. 'There are seven job descriptions in the nursery rhyme but only six names on the scroll,' he said. 'Who's the king?'

Scott frowned. Emily wrote *king* in her notebook and circled it in red. She didn't know either.

But suddenly Jack thought of the answer to his own question. He was so excited he almost inhaled the gobstopper which he'd just put back in his mouth. He took it out again. 'It's King *Arthur*, of course! His name doesn't need to be on the scroll because everyone knows who he is already.'

'You're obsessed with King Arthur these days!' Scott laughed. 'Repeat after me. *We are not on a quest to find the Holy Grail or Excalibur*!'

'Speak for yourself,' Jack replied. 'I can quest if I want to!'

Scott shrugged. He was quite sure the king in the *Keepers of the Key* rhyme wasn't King Arthur. For a start, if it was, he would have received loads of replies to his question on the Arthurian Legends website. But he'd only received one, and it was pretty useless. It was from someone who called himself Sangreal:

To Mad Jack: Send me a private message to tell me what you know, and I can help you.

Yeah, right! Scott had thought. He was far too smart to start sending private messages to people he didn't know! It sounded like the guy was just fishing for information anyway. He'd deleted the message.

Emily was still frowning at her notebook. 'We've got two of the six pieces of the puzzle – the Goff pattern and the Trevithick pattern. Now we just need to find the patterns for the other four families.' She smiled up at Scott and Jack. 'Let's start with the Smuggling Carters.'

There was a long silence.

'Well?' Emily prompted.

'Well what?' Jack asked.

'I think Em's asking whether we happen to have any mysterious Carter family heirlooms with weird Celtic knot designs on them,' Scott said.

'Exactly!' Emily confirmed. 'It's probably on something that's been handed down through the generations – like a gold watch or a family Bible or something.'

Scott and Jack looked at each other and shook their heads.

'I'll phone Dad and see if he knows of anything,' Scott said. 'He's always digging up other people's ancient relics. He's bound to have some from our own family too.'

For once Scott managed to get through to Dad first time. It was evening in Cambodia, where Leo Carter was enjoying a cold beer at the end of a long, hot day's work, excavating the ruins of an ancient temple. He was delighted to hear from Scott and Jack.

They chatted for a while, but when Scott started to quiz his dad on the subject of family heirlooms he was no help at all.

'There were some bits and pieces up in the attic at the old house,' he explained. 'But after we lost your mum in the car crash, I threw the whole lot away. I couldn't bear the memories.'

'But it's things from the Carter side of the family we're after, not Mum's stuff,' Scott pointed out.

'I know,' Dad sighed. 'But I was in such a state that I didn't exactly stop to check what was what.'

Scott knew he might as well give up. He'd only been four at the time, but he remembered Dad storming around the house after Mum died, chucking boxes in a skip.

'We could try asking Aunt Kate,' Jack suggested after Scott had hung up.

As if on cue, Aunt Kate wandered into the living room, looking for some notes she'd mislaid for the latest soppy romantic novel she was writing. 'Ask Aunt Kate what?' she asked.

'We're doing some research on our Carter family roots,' Scott explained. 'We wondered if there were any old heirlooms that had been handed down.'

Aunt Kate looked over her glasses and smiled. 'I'm sorry, I can't help much with that. I'm not a Carter, I'm a Trelawney. My older sister, Jennifer, married your dad's father, William Carter. That's your grandfather, of course. William and Jenny met at high school in Carrickstowe . . .'

'Where did the Carters used to live?' Scott's hopes were up again. The Carter pattern could be hidden somewhere in their old house, just as the Goff pattern had been carved into the fireplace at Stone Cottage. But the hope didn't last long.

'The Carters had a lovely old house over near Tregower,' Aunt Kate said. 'But I'm afraid it burned down soon after William and Jenny had married and moved away to London. Such a shame.' She found her notes on the coffee table and picked them up. 'Why don't you give your granddad a call? He might be able to help. I'll find you the number.'

It was a good idea. And they didn't have any others, so Scott made the call. It was early morning in Canada – which is where Gran and Granddad had lived since they'd retired – but luckily they were up, eating breakfast on their lake-view balcony.

As Gran chatted about all the family news, Scott tried not to think about the body-blow his phone credit was taking with twenty-minute calls to Cambodia and Canada in one morning. When Gran paused for breath, he quickly asked to speak to Granddad about Carter family history.

Granddad had lots to talk about too. Unfortunately, his favourite subjects were *Match of the Day* and Heinz tomato soup – the two things he missed most since moving overseas – rather than his proud Cornish heritage. And he didn't have a clue about any heirlooms with Celtic knot patterns.

Another dead end! Scott thought. But just as he was about to say goodbye, Granddad came up trumps.

'You might find something at the old fuggy hole!' he said.

Eight

Following Another Lead

'The fuggy hole?' Scott repeated his grandfather's words. 'What's that?'

'It's a little cave in the cliff over by West Rock Beach. It's beneath a tumbledown old shepherd's hut,' Granddad explained. 'It was supposed to be one of the places the Carters used to stash their smuggled loot in the old days. We had a great den in there when I was a lad.' Granddad chuckled to himself. 'Funny! I haven't thought about that old fuggy hole in years.'

A few minutes later, Scott said goodbye and hung up. He told Jack and Emily what Granddad had said.

'*Fuggy hole?*' Jack snorted. 'That's a weird name. Are you sure he wasn't pulling your leg?'

'No, it's real,' Emily said. 'It's a nickname for a *fogou*. That's a kind of manmade cave built in the Stone Age. There are a few of them in Cornwall.'

Scott grinned. 'Well, it sounds like the perfect place to find the Carter pattern. Think about it! The other two patterns we've found are in places connected with the family's job. The Goff pattern is on the fireplace that was in the blacksmith's forge. The Trevithick pattern is painted on their fishing boats. So it makes sense that the pattern for a family of smugglers will be in their hideaway.'

'And I think I know the old shepherd's hut he means,' Emily added, excitedly.

Jack jumped up. 'What are we waiting for?' He did a Usain Bolt lightning-bolt mime. 'Full speed ahead to West Rock Beach!'

Emily laughed. 'You might want to change out of your dressing-gown first!' She looked at her watch. 'If we go now we should be back in time for my shift in the spinning tent.'

But when they opened the front door, the friends were almost bowled over by the raging wind that was now storming across the island with the rain in its teeth.

They slammed the door shut again. West Rock Beach was a long cycle ride across South Moor. Even Jack had to admit it might be worth waiting until the worst of the gale had blown over.

'I've got an idea,' Emily said. 'Let's follow up another lead. According to the rhyme, one of the other keepers was a priest. And where do priests work?'

'Er, churches?' Jack ventured, wondering whether this was one of Emily's trick questions.

'Exactly,' Emily said. She opened the door again and pointed down Church Lane.

The square stone tower of St Michael's loomed through the rain, only about a hundred metres away at the bottom of the hill.

'Good idea,' Scott said. 'There's bound to be a record of all the previous priests. We should be able to find out who it was in 1755 when the scroll was written.'

Jack was already pulling on his cagoule and wellies. 'Let's do it! We'll save the fuggy hole for tomorrow.'

One splashy dash down the hill later and the friends were pushing open the heavy wooden door that led into the church.

The cloudy skies meant that very little sunlight filtered through the stained glass windows, but the lamps along the thick stone walls cast pools of warm golden light over the gleaming oak pews and brass candlesticks. Emily breathed in the familiar smell of musty hymn books and polish.

The friends all jumped and looked round as the church was suddenly filled with a tornado of sound. A man with a shaved head, wearing a long brown robe, belted with a cord, was sitting at the huge organ, hammering away at the pedals and keys like something out of *The Muppet Show*.

'That's lucky!' Emily shouted over the noise, which she now recognized as a rock remix of *All Things Bright and Beautiful*. 'I'm sure Colin will help us find the church records.'

Colin Warnock, the young curate, had helped the friends on more than one occasion – although whether he'd actually *known* he was assisting with an investigation was another matter.

The last chords reverberated around the rafters.

When he looked round and saw the friends standing behind him, Colin stood up and smiled. 'Don't worry. I've not decided to run away and join a monastery,' he said, gesturing at his monk's habit. 'I'm dressed as a Celtic monk for History Week.' He crawled under the organ and began adjusting one of the pedals. 'So, what can I do for you?' he asked over his shoulder.

'Do you know who was the priest of this church in 1755?' Jack asked, getting straight to the point as always.

Colin twisted round, looked up and raised his

eyebrows. 'Not off the top of my head. I only came to St Michael's three years ago.'

'We thought there might be some records . . .' Scott explained.

'Of course.' Colin straightened up, brushing dust off the knees of his robe. 'Come and have a look in the vestry. There's a book that lists all the clergy of St Michael's, right back to the time of the Norman Invasion.'

'1066!' Jack said, showing off the one date in history he could remember.

'Top marks!' Colin laughed, as he led the friends under an arch and through a door at the side of the church. They entered a small room that was a cross between a changing room, an office and a store cupboard. 'So, why the sudden interest in St Michael's?'

'Oh, we're doing a project on local history,' Emily said vaguely. It was true, after all; they were uncovering the history of the Keepers of the Key scroll and it *was* turning out to be a major project.

Colin took a key from a hook and unlocked a drawer in an old desk. He took out the biggest book Jack had ever seen. At first he thought it was a Bible, but as Colin opened the cracked brown leather covers and began to turn the yellowing pages, he saw that it was filled with dates and names.

'Now, let's see, 1755 you say?' Colin muttered. The friends peered over his shoulder as he ran his finger down a page. 'Here we are!' He stopped at a line of faded brown copperplate handwriting. 'From 1748 to 1755 the priest was Josiah Lugg.'

Colin was about to clap the book shut when Scott spoke up. 'Can I just have another look?' He flipped back through the pages and saw the same name over and over again. Almost all the priests before Josiah Lugg were also Luggs. Going into the Church was obviously a family tradition. But *after* 1755 it was a different story. There were Polperrows and Martins and Chegwins, but no more Luggs. It was as if the family had ceased to exist.

'Do you know anything about Josiah Lugg?' Emily asked Colin.

The curate shook his head. 'Sorry. But I can show you his tombstone if you like.' He led the friends back into the nave and down the aisle between the pews. 'A lot of the old clergy have tombstones set into the floor. . . Ah, yes, here it is.'

Scott, Jack and Emily knelt to inspect the stone. They glanced at the simple inscription – *Josiah Lugg, 1721–55. Priest of this Parish, 1748–55* – but really all three were searching for something quite different: the intertwining lines of a Celtic knot pattern. There were some faint marks in one corner. For a moment Emily thought that was it – but closer inspection revealed it to be the ferny whorls of a small fossil embedded in the ancient rock.

Colin checked his watch. 'Got to run! I'm due back at the common to give a History Week talk about Celtic Christianity.'

They were walking towards the door together when Colin suddenly stopped. 'I just remembered. There's a load of old stuff that got cleared out of the Old Rectory when it was modernized a few years ago. Some of it goes back centuries. It's mostly books and personal letters that belonged to the previous clergy. You might find something belonging to Josiah Lugg . . .'

'Where?' Emily interrupted, almost too excited to speak. She could think of nothing better than conducting a fingertip search through boxes of old papers. She was certain she'd find a precious gem of evidence which would lead to a vital breakthrough in the investigation. She had her magnifying glass and her evidence bags in her satchel. She was ready to get to work.

'Up in the bell tower,' Colin said. 'There's a room halfway up. It's rather a dumping ground, to be honest. You're welcome to stay and have a look. It's a bit poky up there, though. Might be best to go up one at a time.' He pointed towards a little arched door in the corner. 'Just through there and up the stairs.'

Emily had her hand on the doorknob before he'd even finished the sentence!

Nine

A Discovery in the Graveyard

Jack watched Emily disappear through the little door, Drift at her heels, as always.

He grinned at Scott. 'Looks like Em's taking first shift in the tower then. Rather her than me! Rummaging through a load of old junk – *bor-ing!*' He stuck his hands in his pockets. 'What are we going to do? We don't need to go back to History Week until after lunch.' He thought for a moment. 'Talking of lunch, we could call in at Dotty's for a pizza?'

'It's only eleven o'clock!' Scott laughed. 'I've got a better idea. Let's have a look round the graveyard.'

'Ooh goody!' Jack clapped his hands in mock excitement. 'That sounds like fun!' He paused for a beat. 'Not!' he added.

Scott shoved his brother on the arm. 'I didn't just mean for something to do. The graves of all the old Castle Key families are here. Remember we saw them when we were looking for the Pendragon tomb during Operation Compass? We might spot some more of those Celtic knot patterns and find our missing Keepers of the Key.'

Jack stood in the doorway and eyed the outside world with suspicion. The rain wasn't only belting down from the sky, it was surfing on the wind and cascading from the overhanging branches of the trees that sheltered the graveyard. If it got any wetter they'd have to evolve gills to breathe. It would be warm and dry at Dotty's Tea Rooms. He cupped his hand to his ear. 'What's that I hear? Oh, yes, it's a Super Special pizza with extra chilli and pineapple. It's calling to me!'

Scott laughed. 'Just a quick look. We can't just go and leave Emily here on her own, anyway. And you never know, we might find the Smuggling Carter family graves.'

Jack was tempted. He was always keen to find out more about his smuggling ancestors, but not quite tempted enough. 'We could look tomorrow.'

Scott tried again. 'Just imagine the look on Emily's face if we find a massive clue on our own.'

Jack grinned. That had finally tipped the balance. Out-investigating Emily was *always* worth it! He pulled up the hood of his waterproof and stepped out into the deluge.

The boys soon found the Trevithick graves, huddled together near the southern wall of the graveyard, as if yearning to be close to the sea in death as in life. To Scott and Jack's great delight, the Celtic knot pattern they'd seen on the fishing boats was woven into a decorative border around the tops of all the gravestones. It was chipped away in places, blotched with moss and bird droppings, but there it was, as if keeping watch over every Trevithick skeleton.

'Look at the dates on this gravestone!' Jack said from deep under his hood. He read out loud. '*John Trevithick, 1724 to 1755. Died at sea.*' He shivered as rain dripped into his wellies. 'Must have been dangerous being a fisherman in those days.'

Scott joined him, gazing down at the inscription. 'I can't see any other Trevithicks who were around in 1755. This John must have been the one who signed the scroll.' He snapped some photos of the headstone with his phone camera. 'Let's look for Carters now.'

But this time they drew a blank. There were no Carter graves to be seen. 'There's a chapel over in Tregower,' Scott remembered. 'Aunt Kate said that's where the Carter house used to be. They're probably buried there.'

They couldn't find any graves for the Carrow family either.

'Pizza?' Jack said, hopefully. 'Let's go and give Emily a shout.'

Scott looked around. While they'd been searching, the rain had eased to a fine drizzle and a dense fog had rolled in from the sea. He was about to agree that it was time to knock off, when he noticed another group of graves tucked away behind a stand of pine trees near the tower, the headstones looming out of the mist as if floating in a white sea. He walked across to take a look and started reading the names: *David White, Sarah White, Margaret White . . .*

He rubbed a patch of damp lichen from one of the stones with his thumb. And then from another. 'Jack! Over here!' he yelled.

Jack had almost reached the church door. Reluctantly he turned and jogged back. 'What?' he demanded.

Scott pointed at the nearest of the White headstones. 'What can you see?'

Jack squinted at the stones. 'A Celtic knot pattern!'

Scott grinned. 'If that doesn't match a segment of the tapestry in the secret room, you can tell my friends I've changed my name to Ermintrude!'

'Don't give me ideas!' Jack joked. 'So whose graves are these?'

'The Whites,' Scott said. 'It looks like the family plot. *White* must be one of the two names we can't read on the scroll.'

Instantly, the boys both began to run through the *Keepers of the Key* rhyme under their breath. '*Smuggler, smith, hunter, priest. Farmer, fisherman, king!*' they chorused.

'Of course!' Jack shouted. 'The Whites are the *farmers*. Mr and Mrs White still live at Roshendra Farm, don't they? We've been there loads of times.'

Scott held up his hand for a high-five. 'One more piece of the puzzle falls into place. Quick! Let's get some photos of the pattern. I'm ready for that pizza now too.' He looked up, wondering why Jack had suddenly gone quiet. Surely he hadn't already sloped off towards the café. But then he saw him standing motionless, staring at one of the old headstones.

'I've found the man who signed the scroll,' Jack said without looking up. His voice quavered. 'Samuel White. Born 1736.'

'Great, let's get a picture to show Emily,' Scott said.

Jack didn't move a muscle.

'Why are you gawping at that headstone like you've seen a ghost? I know we're in a graveyard and it's a bit spooky with all the fog and everything, but . . .'

'1755,' Jack murmured.

Scott nodded impatiently. 'Yep, that's the year on the scroll.'

'It's also the year Samuel White died,' Jack said. 'He was born in 1736. That means he was only nineteen.'

'That's sad,' Scott said, wondering why Jack had suddenly come over all sensitive and serious. Perhaps hunger was giving him a funny turn. The sooner he got that pizza, the better.

'It's the same year that John Trevithick died,' Jack whispered. '*And* Josiah Lugg.'

Finally Scott caught on. 'That's weird!' he said. 'Three of the Keepers dying in the same year.' Suddenly fear shot through him like a jet of iced water. 'No,' he murmured. 'It's *four*, not three. I just remembered. Thomas Goff died in 1755 too. It was in the deeds.'

Even Scott wasn't going to try to pass this one off as a coincidence.

There was something very creepy going on. And now Scott had the peculiar feeling they were being watched. For a moment he even thought he heard the soft tread of footsteps on the wet grass behind him, but when he spun round there was no one there.

It seemed Jack could feel it too. He backed away from the grave, throwing terrified glances over his shoulders, as if expecting demonic creatures to crawl out of the mist, reaching out their scrawny, scabrous arms to drag him down under the earth.

'It's like there's a curse on the Keepers of the Key,' Jack whispered. 'And we might just have re-awakened it.'

Ten

Dark Forces in the Tower

Meanwhile, in the bell tower, Emily ran up the spiral staircase, its stone steps worn to spoon-shaped hollows by a thousand years of climbing feet. She came out in a small room, dark but for shafts of light from a pair of arched windows as narrow as arrow slits. She flicked on an ancient-looking light switch. A bare bulb, hanging from a wire that had been tacked across the ceiling, buzzed into life.

Emily surveyed the scene. It looked like the leftovers from a jumble sale. Racks and boxes were stuffed with costumes for Christmas nativity plays and Sunday School pantomimes. Robin Hood's green feathered cap and Aladdin's lamp jostled for space with a pair of angel wings and the back end of a donkey. A cloak of gold and purple brocade and a pair of sequined velvet pantaloons spilled from a trunk marked *Three Wise Men*.

On the other side of the room, boxes of books and papers had been piled against the wall.

While Drift investigated some interesting mouse-related smells in the corner, Emily set to work. But as soon as she lifted a sheaf of papers from the first box she was engulfed by clouds of dust and she started to cough and sneeze. Undeterred, she reached into her shoulder bag, took out a paper face mask – the sort worn by surgeons doing operations – and hooked the loops over her ears. She always kept the mask handy in her investigation kit, in case she needed to examine a crime scene contaminated with chemical or biological hazards. This was the first time she'd had to use it.

She began sifting through centuries of letters, religious pamphlets, shopping lists and sheet music. One priest had left a volume of bad poetry, another his collection of cat photographs. Sitting cross-legged on the floor, Emily pulled yet another box towards her. It was starting to feel like a hopeless task. How would she ever find anything belonging to Josiah Lugg in this chaos? She reached in and pulled out a small notebook, bound in brown scaly leather. It was fastened with a lock, like a secret diary, but when she ran her thumb under it, the strap crumbled to dust. As soon as the book fell open, she knew she'd hit the jackpot.

Emily stared at the words written inside the cover: *Josiah Lugg, 1755.*

The right man! The right year! Breathless with excitement, she began to turn the tissue-thin pages. There were plans for sermons and notes about meetings with parishioners. There were even reminders to talk to someone about the leak in the church roof.

There was nothing about secret societies, hidden objects or mysterious patterns . . .

Emily was about to toss the notebook aside in disappointment when she came to the last few pages. The small, neat writing grew bigger and bigger and began to wander over the paper, up and down and diagonally, and then in swoops and swirls like contours on a map. There were passages that seemed to be in code, and words scored out so violently that the nib of the pen had torn the paper. Inkblots spattered every page. Emily could only read odd phrases here and there.

Dark forces have gathered around us . . . they have harnessed the wrath of nature . . .

There was a date at the top of the page: *10th November, 1755.* According to the inscription on his tombstone, Lugg had died by the end of the year. *That means he only had a few weeks to live when he wrote this stuff*, she thought. Perhaps the poor man had been delirious with a raging fever. That might explain the random weirdness.

More lines were squashed upside-down in the margin.

All have perished who would protect our ancient knowledge. The great secret our families have kept for a thousand years will be lost. I must try to preserve it but I am not long for this world . . .

Emily stared at the words and gasped. *Ancient Knowledge? Great Secret?*

Could this be more than the crazed ramblings of a dying man? Suddenly she spotted something that made her heart miss a beat. Written backwards across the page were the words, *Keepers of the Key*.

'Yes!' Emily breathed.

She heard a noise and glanced up, thinking it was Drift still rooting around in the corner. But Drift was standing with one ear – the white one with brown spots – perked up in Listening Formation. He had heard it too. Someone was coming up the stairs.

It must be Scott or Jack, Emily thought. She was about to call out, but the words stuck in her throat. This wasn't one of the boys. The steps were slow and shuffling. The breathing rattled and wheezed. And now, as the unknown person reached the top of the stairs, the shadow of a figure was cast onto the wall: short, hunched, hooded and cloaked.

Emily felt the hairs prickle on the back of her neck.

Old Bob's warning rang in her ears: *Beware the hooded man!*

She shrank back amongst the boxes and tried to block Lugg's words from her mind. *Dark forces have gathered . . . All have perished . . .*

Now the figure was entering the room. It was holding a huge metal key!

The figure stopped and pushed back its hood – to reveal the red-veined face of a stout, and rather unfit, man in a long, dripping waterproof cape. 'I swear those stairs get steeper every week!' he chuckled to himself.

Suddenly the man noticed Emily and Drift. 'Oh, hello there.' He wiped raindrops from his glasses. 'Young Emily Wild from The Lighthouse, isn't it? Don't mind me. I've just come to wind the clock.' He waved the key towards the corner of the room where a flight of wooden stairs, no wider than a stepladder, led up through a hole in the ceiling. 'It's up on the next floor. More bloomin' steps! And my gammy leg's playing up something chronic!'

Emily could hardly stop herself from bursting into hysterical giggles of relief. She recognized the old man. Harry Mabbutt lived by himself in a tiny cottage near the church and was always out doing odd jobs: mowing the grass in the graveyard, fixing broken guttering, sweeping leaves from the path.

He wasn't a 'dark force'!

85

Harry noticed Emily staring at the key. He held it up. 'The clock mechanism's locked inside a special cabinet.'

With that, he began to puff his way up the wooden stairs.

What was that funny word Jack made up? Emily thought as she watched him go. *Frimbly. That was it. Well, that was definitely a frimbly moment!*

She picked up Lugg's notebook and continued to read.

She found the *Keepers of the Key* rhyme written in miniature letters in a tiny spiral at the bottom of a page. Next to it were six names, each followed by a series of numbers: *Daniel, Luke, Ezra, Matthew, Jeremiah, Peter.* Were they the six Keepers? No, that couldn't be right, because she knew that two of the Keepers were Thomas Goff and Josiah Lugg – and neither *Thomas* nor *Josiah* was listed. And what about the numbers? Phone numbers? No, that was silly, they didn't have phones in 1755!

Emily stared at the names. They seemed familiar somehow. Suddenly she laughed out loud at herself. Of course: she was in a church after all. The six names were all books of the Bible. And the numbers were chapters and verses.

She'd seen a small pocket Bible in one of the boxes. She opened it and flipped through the pages to find the first verse on the list: Daniel, Chapter Three, Verse Thirteen. She read it under her breath. It was all about someone called Nebuchadnezzar summoning people with names like Shadrach and Abednego.

She tried another of the citations. Luke, Chapter Eleven, Verse Forty-four. This time it was about men walking over unmarked graves without knowing it.

Emily sighed. She had no idea what Lugg was getting at. She turned the last page and saw that on the inside of the back cover, he had scribbled the words *Read between the lines, six turns to find.* But what lines? What turns? It seemed Lugg was trying to pass on the secret of the Keepers of the Key puzzle to future generations, but at the same time hide the information from what he called *dark forces.* Was he using the Bible verses as some kind of complicated code?

Emily shivered and realized her fingers were going numb.

She stuffed Josiah Lugg's notebook into her bag, walked across to one of the narrow windows and looked down. It had stopped raining at last but a thick fog now blanketed the world below. It was like looking down on a cloudbank from an aeroplane. As her eyes adjusted, Emily could make out the outlines of trees and bushes as blurry as a watercolour painting. She could see Scott and Jack crouching beside one of the gravestones. She looked beyond the boys to the gate that led out onto Church Lane.

For a moment she thought there was another figure standing there.

A hooded figure in a dark cloak.

Beware the hooded man!

Old Bob's words were back to haunt her once more.

She blinked. The bright white canvas of sky and fog was making pinpricks of light sparkle in front of her eyes.

When she looked again, the shadowy figure had vanished.

Eleven

The Wrath of Nature

Emily shuddered as she turned away from the window. Then she gave herself a shake. 'I'm just spooking myself out with hooded men and dark forces!' she said out loud. 'I'll be seeing Dementors and ghosts next!' She bent and gave Drift a reassuring hug. It was probably just Colin coming back for something he'd forgotten. Or maybe Harry Mabbut had left by another staircase and was on his way out.

But still, she couldn't fly down the spiral stairs fast enough. She pushed open the door at the bottom of the bell tower and barrelled straight into Scott, who was pulling it open from the other side.

'You'll never guess what I found!' Emily cried.

'You'll never guess what we found!' Jack shouted at the same time.

They all laughed.

'Go on, you first,' Emily said.

But Scott made an exaggerated bow. 'Ladies first!'

Emily hated being called a lady but she was more than happy to go first. She whipped the notebook out of her bag. 'Look! It belonged to Josiah Lugg.' As she brandished the book, a loose page fell out. Caught on a draught, it floated underneath a pew. Drift ran and fetched it back in his mouth. Scott took the piece of paper. As he was handing it back to Emily, he noticed a doodle in the corner. He looked closer. It was a small Celtic knot design.

'Good find, Em!' he said. 'The Lugg family pattern.'

Emily stared down at the page. 'I hadn't even seen that,' she murmured, kicking herself for having missed something so important. 'But there's loads of other stuff in here too, about secrets and dark forces, and there are some Bible verses which are some kind of code about finding six turns . . .'

Emily heard a noise behind her and turned to see Harry Mabbutt coming out of the door from the tower.

'That'll keep the clock going for another week,' he said. 'Now, let's see how the drains are coping with all this rain.'

The friends watched as Harry shuffled down the aisle, with a rustle of waterproofs and squeak of wellies.

'So, what did you two find?' Emily asked. 'I saw you in the graveyard.' She was just wondering whether to mention the shadowy figure by the gate, when she was interrupted by a chorus of extreme gurgling from Jack's stomach.

'Uh-oh!' Jack laughed. 'That's red alert! It means I'll self-destruct if I don't get pizza within the next fifteen minutes.' He began to make for the door. 'Come on. This is an emergency! We'll tell you what we found when we get to Dotty's.'

—

Dotty's café was packed. Crowds of people had called in on their lunch break from History Week duties. A large table of off-duty Saxon peasants was tucking into fish and chips. At the counter, a posse of Cornish warriors was debating whether Manchester United should have been given a penalty against Liverpool last night. Some of the warriors, it seemed, had been sampling the ale and mead during the Ancient Brewing Techniques demonstration. Two druids and a monk in black robes were sitting in the corner checking their text messages.

Scott, Jack and Emily squeezed round a small table at the back and ordered Cokes and pizzas. While they waited the boys told Emily the information they'd garnered in the graveyard.

'We've identified another of the Keepers,' Scott said. 'Samuel White. He has to be the farmer in the nursery rhyme. There's a pattern on his grave and everything.'

'And wait till you hear this,' Jack chimed in. 'It'll freak you out!' He paused theatrically. 'Samuel White and John Trevithick both died in 1755.'

Emily's eyes widened in surprise. 'That's the same year as Josiah Lugg!'

Scott nodded. '*And* Thomas Goff. All four Keepers we know about died in the same year.'

Jack took a slurp from the Coke Dotty had just handed him. 'And none of the men was very old,' he added. The whole everybody-dead-in-one-year thing had given him a serious case of the heebie-jeebies when they were standing in the swirling fog in the graveyard, but it didn't seem half as creepy in the warm, friendly café with pizzas just arriving at the table. All that stuff about ancient curses and demonic creatures seemed silly now. He decided not to bring it up again in case Scott started winding him up about it. Instead, he dolloped ketchup on his pizza and tucked in.

'Perhaps they all caught some really infectious fatal disease,' Emily suggested. 'Like smallpox or something.'

Scott took a bite of pizza and shook his head. 'John

Trevithick's gravestone said he died at sea.'

Emily passed her last piece of pizza to Drift, who was waiting patiently under the table, pushed her plate aside and began to write up the latest developments in her notebook. She chewed the end of her silver pen. 'So, what's our next move?'

Scott thought for a moment. 'I think it's time for a spot of history . . .'

Emily looked at her watch and grimaced. 'Oh, no, you're right! I'm going to be late!' She started gathering up her things. 'I've got to go home and get changed. I told Mum I'd help with the spinning again this afternoon.' She mimed a yawn.

Scott laughed. 'OK, but I wasn't talking about History Week. I meant the history of what happened in Castle Key in 1755. We need to do some research in the library and find out how all those men died. It might be important.'

History . . . library . . . research . . . Jack felt his eyes start to glaze over. He did want to know what had happened to the men but Scott was making it sound far too much like school work. But suddenly he remembered something. 'We've got to get back to the common now as well,' he told Scott. 'Remember, we're in the tug-of-war final this afternoon.' He pretended to rub tears from his eyes. 'What a shame! There won't be time for any in-depth research today.'

Emily grinned. 'The library's open late on Tuesdays.

93

Meet you there at six o'clock.'

'Can't wait!' Jack muttered weakly.

The friends met at the small library on the high street just after six. They headed straight for the local history section and took down all the books they could find about Castle Key in the eighteenth century. They sat round a large table, with the pile of books in the middle, and began to read about tin mining and taxation and religious reforms. At least, Scott and Emily began to read. Jack propped a large book in front of his face so he could daydream in peace about being a Knight of the Round Table. King Arthur was just dubbing him on both shoulders with his sword and saying *Arise, Sir Jack!* when he was rudely interrupted by a shout of, 'Ker-ching!'

Scott was jabbing his finger at a book. 'The Lisbon Tsunami, 1755,' he said. 'That's our year!'

'Lisbon?' Emily asked. 'But isn't that in Portugal?'

Scott nodded. 'It says here that a massive earthquake in Lisbon triggered a tsunami in the Atlantic Ocean. A three-metre-high tidal wave hit the coast of Cornwall.'

Jack was impressed. 'Wow! I didn't know there'd ever been a tsunami in Britain.'

Emily could hardly contain her excitement. 'Do you think the Keepers could all have drowned in the tsunami?'

'Yes, listen to this!' Scott cleared his throat and read from the book.

'*Shortly after two in the afternoon on 1ˢᵗ November, 1755, the first wave hit the island of Castle Key. Local man, Ezekiel Nancarrow, was out trapping rabbits on the clifftop when he raised the alarm that a ship had run aground on the rocks in Key Bay and was sinking fast. He ran down to the harbour and enlisted the help of four other men who were in the Ship and Anchor. Together they rowed out in the fishing boat,* Queen of the May, *which belonged to one of the group, whose name was . . .*' Scott paused and looked from Emily to Jack and back to Emily again, '*John Trevithick.*'

Emily gasped. 'That's one of our Keepers!'

'Result!' Jack whispered.

Scott nodded and went on reading. '*Battling towering seas, the men rowed to the wreck three times to rescue the stranded crew and passengers of the Dutch vessel – including many women and children. But on the fourth attempt, disaster struck. A second wave swept in and the* Queen of the May *was lost with all hands, including . . .*' Scott beat out a drum roll with his palms on the edge of the table, '*. . . John Trevithick, Samuel White, Thomas Goff and Nathan Carter.*'

Emily shook her head in amazement. 'So that was the end of four of the Keepers!' She began frantically writing down the details in her notebook, pausing only to wipe away a smudge of silver ink with her thumb.

Suddenly Scott had an idea. 'Have you got a photo of the scroll in your notebook, Em?' he asked.

'Of course! That's our primary evidence.' She turned the page to where she had stuck the print-out of the photo.

Scott held it up to the light for a moment. 'Hmmm,' he murmured. 'Just as I thought.'

'What?' Emily demanded.

Scott made a wise-and-mysterious face. '*Five* of the Keepers went down in that boat, not four!'

'How do you figure that out?' Jack demanded.

'The third name on the scroll is *Nancarrow*, not Carrow. It just came to me when I saw Emily wipe away ink from her notebook. There's an inkblot over the *Nan* part.'

Emily peered at the photo of the scroll. 'Oh, yes! I can see it now. Brilliant work!'

Scott was looking far too pleased with himself for Jack's liking. 'Hang on!' Jack said. 'What about Josiah Lugg? He wasn't killed in the tsunami.'

'Well, he *was* a priest,' Scott pointed out. 'I guess he wasn't boozing in the pub with the other guys when Ezekiel Nancarrow went looking for helpers.'

Emily took Lugg's notebook from her bag and ran her hand over the cracked leather cover. Poor Josiah Lugg! People probably didn't know what caused tsunamis back then. A monster tidal wave had simply swept in from nowhere and wiped out all five of the other

Keepers of the Key in one fell swoop! No wonder the priest believed that dark forces had somehow harnessed the wrath of nature.

And in a few more weeks, Lugg himself had died. Knowing that he was dying, he must have feared that the great secret that the Keepers had guarded for so many years would be lost forever. Maybe, Emily figured, the secret was handed down from father to son – but because all the men had died so young, they hadn't passed it on to the next generation in time. So Lugg had started to write down clues to preserve it for the future.

'Don't worry! The secret won't be lost,' Emily murmured. 'Not if we have anything to do with it!'

Twelve

A Close Shave at the Fuggy Hole

When Scott woke up the following morning every bone in his body was aching. The Celtic Britons had defeated the Saxons in the tug-of-war final yesterday, but it had been a long and hard-fought battle. He had muscle pains in places he didn't even know he had muscles.

He gave up on trying to move. Instead he lay completely still and mulled over Operation Key. They'd made good progress so far. They had the names of all six Keepers and knew what had happened to them in 1755.

But on the downside, they still only had four of the six pieces of the Celtic knot; the Carter and Nancarrow family patterns were yet to be found. And, of course, there was the minor detail that they had no idea what to do with the six pieces when they had them all! Those odd messages in Josiah Lugg's notebook might hold some clues, but first they had to crack his Bible code puzzles to find out what they meant.

Scott guessed the patterns would eventually fit together to form a key to open something and find the *object of great importance* that Old Bob had told them about.

But what it was and where it was remained a mystery.

—

Today's plan was to follow up on the boys' granddad's lead and check out the fuggy hole under the derelict shepherd's hut at West Rock Beach. The friends were certain they'd find the Carter pattern in the cave the smuggling Carters had used as their hideaway. They'd decided on an early start; Scott and Jack met Emily and Drift on the village green at nine o'clock.

Together they cycled along the winding single-track road that followed the southern coast of the island. The rain had ceased, but morning mist still shrouded the sea to their left. The sun was breaking through the cloud, sparkling on the rain-drenched drifts of heather and gorse on the moorland that stretched away to the right.

The abandoned shepherd's hut sat on top of the low rocky cliff at the far end of West Rock Beach. It was perilously close to the edge and, with its crumbling stone walls, looked at if it had grown right out of the cliff face.

The friends turned down the overgrown path from the road and propped their bikes up against the side of the hut. They peeped inside. It was clear that the hut hadn't sheltered any shepherds for a long time; it was now home only to a colony of gannets. Half the roof was missing, but parts of the wooden platform that had served as hayloft-slash-bedroom were still in place, and there were rusty old iron hooks and feeding troughs hanging from the walls.

Then they walked along the steep cliff path that zigzagged down to the beach. Halfway down, Scott looked up and spotted the mouth of a single small cave in the rock face about ten metres below the hut. 'That must be the fuggy hole!' he said.

Jack frowned. 'You'd need proper rock-climbing gear to get up to that from here. Or you could abseil down from the top, I suppose . . .'

'There must be another way down,' Emily said, as they walked back up the path. 'Your granddad said they used to muck about in there as kids. I'm sure they didn't have abseiling equipment.'

But a fingertip search of the area around the hut failed to reveal any other route to the cave.

Scott was wondering whether he had enough credit left to phone Canada and ask Granddad how to get to the fuggy hole, when Jack came up with an idea. Maybe there was a tunnel to the cave *inside* the hut. That was just the kind of thing smugglers would have built! He hurried inside to investigate. It wasn't a pleasant job!

Gannets and gulls really don't get the concept of personal hygiene, Jack thought. Every surface was coated with stinky white droppings as thick and hard as cement. He was about to retreat outside for some fresh air when he pushed aside a pile of stones and glimpsed the edge of a curved slab of wood beneath.

'In here!' he cried.

Scott, Emily and Drift ran to his side and helped to clear the rubble away. A large round board – like a wooden manhole cover – slowly appeared. Speechless with excitement, the friends heaved it to one side.

It was covering a deep hole.

Emily grabbed her torch from her bag and shone it into the dark space. Rough steps had been hewn from the stone and led down at a steep angle, disappearing inside the cliff.

'Jack, that's genius!' Emily laughed. 'How did you know to look in here?'

'Oh, just a hunch,' Jack said in his super-casual voice. 'When you've got smuggling in your genes like I have, you just know what to look for.'

Scott rolled his eyes at Jack's bragging. He took Emily's spare torch and began to feel his way down the steps. The roof was so low he had to stoop, which made his aching muscles cry out for mercy. Luckily, it wasn't long before the tunnel flattened out and he found himself at the back of a cave the size of a small room. A lozenge of dazzling sunlight shone in through the cave mouth. Scott edged towards it and peeped out. There was an almost vertical drop to the beach and the sea below. He quickly backed away from the edge.

'Wow!' Jack whistled, as he, Emily and Drift joined Scott, who was shining his torch beam slowly around the cave. The walls and ceiling were covered in words scratched into the stone or scrawled with white chalk or red paint. 'Awesome,' Jack breathed. 'To think this has all been in here for hundreds of years.' He noticed a slogan on the ceiling. '*Bill Carter woz 'ere,*' he read out. 'Bill Carter? That must be one of our smuggling ancestors. It might even be from 1755. Oh, yeah! We're bound to find our Celtic knot pattern here somewhere.'

But Scott shook his head. 'I don't think so.' He directed his torch at the words *Elvis Rocks* plastered across the back wall. 'I'm guessing that's Elvis *Presley*. You know, the rock singer? That's more *1955* than *1755*.'

'Yeah,' Emily sighed. 'It says *Bill 4 Jenny 4 Eva* over here.'

Drift looked up from snuffling at a pile of old *Beano* comics and sweet wrappers in the corner.

'What are you saying?' Jack asked.

'Bill's short for William,' Scott explained. 'Granddad is *William* Carter. And Granny is called Jenny. This must be from when she was his girlfriend. And I guess he and his mates were big Elvis fans.'

Jack stared at Scott and Emily, his mouth hanging open as the truth slowly dawned on him. He was frothing with outrage! 'You mean Granddad and his mates daubed their stupid graffiti all over my family's historical heritage? It's, it's, it's . . . mindless vandalism!' he fumed.

Emily and Scott couldn't help laughing. 'You sound like an irate old lady!' Scott said.

But their laughter didn't last long. Jack was right, after all. If the Carter knot pattern had ever been engraved on these walls, it had long since been covered over by generations of graffiti.

They climbed back up the steps through the tunnel. Scott was the first to the top. Stepping up into the hut, he thought he caught sight of a movement near the door. But at the same moment, Drift yelped a high-pitched bark of alarm just behind him. As he stepped back and turned to see what was the matter, an avalanche of timbers cascaded from the wooden platform and crashed to the ground. They landed on the spot where Scott had been standing just milliseconds before. The impact sent up a mushroom cloud of dust and droppings.

There was a cacophony of flapping and squawking as hundreds of startled gannets took flight.

'Phew! That was a close shave!' Jack whistled as he pulled Scott to safety. 'It's like the hut was booby-trapped or something.' He grinned. 'I bet Granddad and his mates left it like that in case enemy gangs tried to get in!'

'Are you OK?' Emily asked Scott, noticing blood trickling from a scratch on his arm. 'You must've caught yourself on one of those nails.' She pointed to three long nails poking out from the wall. It seemed Scott wasn't their first victim. Tufts of yellow-grey sheep's wool and a scrap of thick black cloth were snagged on their rusty points. 'Come on, I've got some antiseptic and plasters in my bag.'

Scott sighed as he sat down on a flat boulder and let Emily tend to his arm. He wasn't having a good day. He hurt all over from the tug-of-war. His arm was stinging – although that was more from Emily's industrial-strength antiseptic than the scratch itself – and there was a kind of woozy cotton-wool feeling in his head. *Must be the shock of almost being buried alive by old planks*, he thought. *It's a good thing Drift warned me with that bark!* He turned to Drift, who was curled up at his side, and gave him a big hug.

Drift licked his hand as if to say, 'Don't mention it!'

Scott gazed out to sea. He could hear Emily and Jack behind him unpacking some blueberry muffins from Jack's backpack for elevenses. He glanced down at the beach far below. Tendrils of sea fog still swirled around the base of the cliffs. *Uh-oh*, Scott thought. *Now I'm seeing things as well!* A figure in a long, black hooded cloak was walking slowly along the sand, like a mediaeval monk or something out of *Lord of the Rings*.

Or just one of the History Week actors out for a walk, he told himself.

He was about to beckon Emily and Jack over to take a look when Emily waved her phone and called out. 'I've just had a text message from Mum. She says Old Bob is allowed visitors from today and he's asked to see us . . .' She looked at her watch. 'Visiting time ends at midday. If we get a move on we could just make it to the hospital in time.'

Scott clambered to his feet. As he walked to his bike he looked back over his shoulder. The hooded figure had disappeared.

Thirteen

The Second Verse

'What does Old Bob want to see *us* for?' Jack asked as they jumped on their bikes. As far as Jack was concerned, being summoned to see an adult usually spelled trouble of some kind.

'I bet he's got some more information about the Keepers of the Key legend,' Emily said excitedly.

Scott was doubtful. The man had been clouted by a low-flying Saxon battle-axe. He almost certainly had other things on his mind than old nursery rhymes – like a massive great bump on his head, for a start. 'Em, promise you won't start grilling Old Bob about the Keepers the second we get there,' he said.

'As if I would!' Emily protested.

Scott grinned at Jack. They'd seen Emily's bedside manner before. It could easily be mistaken for a police interrogation!

The friends raced over the island, across the causeway and into Carrickstowe, making it to the hospital in record time and with seven and a half minutes of visiting time to go.

They had to leave Drift in his basket on Emily's bike, as dogs weren't allowed in the hospital, of course.

'We'll be back soon!' Emily told him, before haring off to catch up with the boys. As they crossed the concourse, she made a detour to the flower stall, grabbed a bunch of carnations and stuffed the money into the florist's hand. 'See!' she puffed, waving the flowers as they hurtled down the corridor. 'I do know how to be nice to patients!'

They found the ward and skidded to a halt next to Old Bob's bed at four minutes to twelve. The old man was propped up on a bank of pillows. He was wearing his threadbare navy blue jumper over a striped pyjama top, and looked just like his normal self – except that his bushy white eyebrows bristled out from under a turban-like bandage instead of his usual woollen cap.

'How are you feeling?' Emily asked sweetly, thrusting the flowers at him.

Old Bob nodded. 'Not too bad.'

'Is your head very painful?' Emily went on. She shot a look at the boys to make sure they'd noticed her caring side.

'Never mind about that. It'll mend,' Old Bob said. 'There's something I need to tell you kids and we haven't got much time. The nurses here are sticklers for rules. They'll chuck you out on the dot of noon.' He looked around as if checking for eavesdroppers. 'I know who hit me over the head,' he said in a hushed voice. Jack, Emily and Scott all leaned in closer to catch Old Bob's words. 'It just came back to me this morning. And it wasn't one of that daft Saxon lot.'

'Who was it?' Emily breathed.

'I don't know his name. I'd never seen him before.'

'But why did he hit you?' Jack put in.

Old Bob shook his head in puzzlement. 'That's what I'd like to know. But I think it had something to do with that old *Keepers of the Key* ditty you were asking me about the other day. That's what I wanted to tell you about.'

Emily looked triumphantly at Jack and Scott. 'I knew it!'

Old Bob glanced along the ward. One of the nurses was on her way. 'This chap in a monk's outfit came over while I was waiting to go into battle,' he said. 'He started asking a lot of questions about whether I knew any old stories about King Arthur hiding relics here. You know, the Holy Grail, that kind of thing. Like I said before, outsiders think the whole of Cornwall is choc-a-bloc with Arthur's cast-offs! So I told him a couple of tall tales – the kind of stuff tourists like. Then he asked me if I'd ever heard of the Keepers of the Key. Funny you should mention that, I said to him, because my three young friends were just asking me about that old rhyme the other day. Which reminds me, I said, I must tell them that I've remembered the second verse. Well, he looked like he'd just got the winning lottery ticket!'

Old Bob took a sip from a glass of water on the bedside table and then went on. 'He asked me what the second verse of the rhyme was, so I told him. Then I turned round to pick up my sword. That's when I felt a wallop on the back of the helmet. Next thing I know I'm in an ambulance! So I wanted to warn you to be on the lookout for him.'

The friends all began to ask questions at once.

'What did he look like?' asked Scott.

'What is the second verse of the rhyme?' asked Emily.

'Can I have those strawberries if you don't want them?' asked Jack.

Old Bob smiled and handed Jack the bowl. 'The man was dressed as a monk in a black robe,' he said. 'He kept his hood pulled down over his face but I'd recognize him anywhere.'

'That explains what you said when you were lying on the battlefield,' Emily said. *'Beware the hooded man!'*

'Yeah,' Jack agreed, biting into a large strawberry. 'It was dead frimbly.'

'You said you'd recognize him anywhere,' Scott prompted. 'How?'

'His hood slipped back at one point and, before he could pull it up again, I caught sight of his eyes.' Old Bob swallowed hard as if still unnerved by the memory. 'Horrible, they were. One black as night. The other milky white like the skin on a rice pudding.'

'Uggh!' Jack said, dropping a strawberry back into the bowl. 'You're putting me off my food here!'

'What about the *Keepers of the Key* rhyme?' Emily interrupted impatiently. The squeak of the nurse's rubber-soled crocs was getting closer. Time was running out. 'You said you'd remembered another verse.'

'That's right. I was thinking about it after you asked me and I remembered my old granny singing it while she was pounding the washing in the tub.' Old Bob began chanting in a soft voice.

'He who would be king,
With all the king's power,
Six turns must make,
From the dungeon to the tower.'

'The dungeon to the tower,' Emily repeated. 'That sounds like it's hidden in the castle.'

'Of course!' Scott said. 'We should have guessed. It's called Key Castle for a start!'

'What's hidden in the tower?' Old Bob asked.

'Visiting time's over!' The nurse's brisk command made them all jump. 'Off you go now! We mustn't tire Mr Trevithick out, must we?'

As the nurse leaned over to plump up his pillows, Old Bob looked over her shoulder. 'Remember what I said. Beware the hooded man!'

Fourteen

Beware the Hooded Man

That night, long after Scott was asleep on the other side of the room, Jack sat up in bed reading.

His bedside lamp cast a pool of amber light. A fat moth bumbled against the bulb. The rain clawed at the windows.

Jack wasn't big on reading as a rule, apart from comics or books that were really funny or dead scary or full of gory facts. But tonight he was on a mission.

He was searching for the Nancarrows, the missing family from the Keepers of the Key scroll. After their visit to Old Bob, he and Scott and Emily had gone back to the church and searched the graveyard, but they'd found no Nancarrow graves later than 1950 – and none of them featured any Celtic knot patterns. They had also searched the phone book. No Nancarrows were listed.

But Jack was sure he'd heard the name somewhere before. He couldn't pin it down, but the more he thought about it the more he was certain it had cropped up in one of their earlier cases. So he'd asked Emily to lend him all her notebooks and now he was combing through them for a mention.

Emily kept her case notebooks locked up in a special safe under her bed. She'd allowed Jack to borrow them for a twenty-four hour period, although only after he'd left a deposit of £3.76 (which happened to be all he had in his pocket) and signed an agreement promising not to let them out of his sight or discuss their contents with anyone else.

He started with Operation Treasure, their first ever case together. No Nancarrows. Then he moved on to Operation Lost Star. No Nancarrows. Jack sighed. Words were swimming in front of his eyes and he still had another ten investigations to go. Even the moth had given up on the light bulb and flown out of the window. He picked up the notebook labelled Operation Gold and began to flick through.

Suddenly he saw it.

5.45 a.m.: Proceeded to Dotty's Tea Rooms to interview Robert Trevithick (a.k.a. Old Bob) about Gull Island . . . Mrs Irene Loveday joined interview at 6.02 a.m. Reported that her grandmother was told by Maud Jenkins that Sally Nancarrow had witnessed John Macy carry an unknown man to the lighthouse in . . .

'Oh yeah!' Jack shouted. 'Gotcha!'

'Whassup?' Scott murmured from under his blankets.

'I've found Nancarrow! Listen to this!' Jack read out the passage from Emily's notebook.

'But Mrs Loveday was talking about something that happened over a hundred years ago – the night the *Empress* sank in Key Bay in 1902,' Scott groaned. 'Go to sleep.'

Jack didn't give up. 'Mrs Loveday might know where Sally Nancarrow's descendants have moved to. They've obviously left the island. I'll pump her for information in the morning.'

Scott sat up. 'No way! You can't be trusted to talk to Mrs Loveday without starting World War Three! I'll talk to her.'

Jack had to admit Scott had a point. For some reason Mrs Loveday had taken a dislike to him from their very first meeting. And if there was one thing Scott was good at (one of the very few things, in Jack's opinion), it was talking to old ladies. 'Alright,' he said reluctantly. 'As long as you don't tell Emily this was *your* brilliant idea!'

Next morning Scott donned his tunic and cloak and set off for the common. He knew that Mrs Loveday was helping out in the weapon stores for History Week. The huge tent was filled with racks and boxes of swords, shields, helmets and other battle supplies. It smelled of damp canvas and sweaty socks, like a cross between Scout camp and the school changing rooms.

Mrs Loveday was busy scrubbing mud off the battle-axes. She was dressed in Cornish Briton costume – a long brown dress and tartan cloak fastened with a metal brooch – but she'd forgotten to remove her pink Disney Princess cycle helmet, which was still perched on top of her grey curls, and she'd added a fruit-patterned nylon apron to protect her dress. It was not, in Scott's opinion, an entirely successful fashion statement.

His first move was to get on the old lady's good side by presenting her with an offering – a cup of tea he'd bought at Dotty's café on the way. He'd had to smuggle the Styrofoam takeaway cup past the History Week organizers under his cloak (only authentic clay or wooden bowls or metal goblets were allowed on site, of course!). Mrs Loveday took a slurp. 'Ooh, you can't beat a proper cuppa!' she sighed.

His second move was to make himself useful. He picked up a cloth and began to polish a sword hilt.

Mrs Loveday beamed at him. 'Such a helpful young man.'

Scott had been racking his brains for a good cover story for asking Mrs Loveday about the Nancarrows, but he needn't have bothered. Mrs Loveday was quite capable of carrying on both sides of a conversation. She started with Old Bob's 'accident'. She folded her arms across her apron. 'Set upon by a gang of hoodies, he was. They must have infiltrated the Saxon army.'

'Saxon hoodies?' Scott asked, struggling to keep a straight face.

'Oh, yes! Old Bob may have had a Nasty Case of Percussion, but he sat up and said, *Beware those hoodies.* I heard him clear as day.'

'Actually, I think he said *Beware the hooded man*,' Scott pointed out.

Mrs Loveday passed him another sword. 'My point exactly! Talking of hoodies, where's that brother of yours?' She glanced around as if worried Jack might leap out and mug her at spear-point.

Scott was tempted to wind Mrs Loveday up by saying that Jack was out stealing lollipops from small children or scribbling on library books. But he decided against it. She'd probably believe him and call the police. Instead he smiled his most charming smile and gently nudged the conversation in the right direction. 'I don't suppose they had hoodies in Castle Key in your day. You must have seen a lot of changes . . .'

Mrs Loveday was delighted with this free ticket to hold forth on one of her favourite topics. Scott did his best to look interested. It was almost twenty minutes before the old lady paused for breath.

Scott was straight in with another nudge. 'I expect some of the old families you remember have left now?'

'Ooh yes. There were the Vances. They moved to a caravan park in Newquay. And the Lintons and the Nancarrows . . .'

'The Nancarrows?' Scott repeated, almost stabbing himself with a sword in his excitement.

'Oh, yes, dear. They were a very old Castle Key family. But they Elevated after the war.'

'*Elevated?*' Scott echoed.

'To Australia.'

'Oh, you mean *emigrated*!'

Mrs Loveday examined the shine on a shield. 'That's right. Emigrated. To run a trout farm.'

'Where did they used to live?'

'Over the shop,' Mrs Loveday said. 'They owned that little fishing tackle store on Pilchard Lane. It was passed down through the generations like a Family Airline. They used to sell hunting supplies as well, but there's no call for that these days . . .'

Scott was so pleased with this information that he

didn't even mention to Mrs Loveday that she might have meant *heirloom*, not *airline*.

He made a show of glancing at his watch and looking surprised at the time. 'So sorry, must rush . . . lovely to talk to you . . .'

—

Meanwhile, Jack was kicking a crushed Fanta can along the high street. He was fed up. Scott had totally hijacked his Nancarrow idea. Emily was busy helping her mum in the spinning tent. What was he supposed to do all morning?

To make matters worse, Old Bob's words – *Beware the hooded man!* – kept buzzing round in his head. But how was he meant to *beware* when the whole island was *swarming* with hooded men? He'd just passed Colin Warnock leading a procession of hooded monks to the church to do a bell-ringing demo. A bunch of white-hooded Celtic druids were on their way into the Ship and Anchor. Then the clock-winder, Harry Mabbutt, shuffled out of the mini-market with a tin of cat food and a packet of Hobnobs, the hood of his waterproof cape pulled up against the rain.

But, as he passed the library, Jack suddenly had one of his brainwaves.

He lobbed the can into a litter bin and hurried inside. *If Josh and Ali at school could see me now, running into a library,* he thought, *they'd be splitting their sides laughing.* But secretly Jack had to admit the library had come in handy in their investigations in all kinds of ways, as well as for finding out about his smuggling roots. He was starting to know his way around!

He took a big book about King Arthur off the shelf.

Jack was still convinced that the Keepers of the Key secret was to do with King Arthur, even if Scott, Emily and Old Bob had laughed at the idea that the Keepers were looking after the Holy Grail or Excalibur. They all seemed to be ignoring the fact that the nursery rhyme went, *farmer, fisherman, hunter, KING.* And what about that second verse Old Bob had remembered? It was all about the king and the king's power! *Hel-lo! How much more obvious can it get?* Jack thought. *If this isn't about King Arthur, I'll eat nothing but Brussels sprouts for a month!*

He turned the pages of the book, searching for some sort of clue as to what exactly the Keepers were guarding and where they'd hidden it. There had to be *something* linking King Arthur to Castle Key island, a name or a person or a place . . .

Then he saw it!

Arthur was the son of Uther Pendragon . . .

Of course! Arthur's family name was *Pendragon.* And there was a Pendragon Manor right here on Castle Key. That was the link! Arthur must have lived there at some point. There was bound to be a clue at the manor. Or even the Keepers' secret hiding place itself.

Jack's heart was pounding with excitement. The only problem was that Pendragon Manor was huge! Where would they even start to look? Then he remembered the ancient disused chapel in the grounds. It was full of old tombs and gravestones and statues – exactly the kind of place important secrets could lie hidden for thousands of years!

He knew he should wait for Scott and Emily, but they might be ages and it was physically impossible *not* to act instantly on a stroke of genius this awesome.

He'd go and find the Holy Grail all by himself.

Jack ran to Stone Cottage, jumped on his bike and rode like the wind.

He was in such a hurry he didn't even take a packed lunch!

Pendragon Chapel was deep in the heart of the ancient woods that surrounded the manor. The path was even more overgrown than Jack remembered. It was boggy, too, after the rain. He propped his bike against a giant oak tree and pushed on through the dripping brambles on foot. At last he came to the small stone building, almost invisible under the vegetation. He pulled away the ivy and pushed open the old wooden door.

Bats swooped down from the rafters. Cobwebs clung to his mouth and nose. A huge black spider scurried across the wall. Jack almost turned and fled, but he steeled himself and crept towards the Pendragon tomb. Along the top lay a young woman carved from marble so white that it glowed ghostly pale in the gloom. *This place,* Jack thought, *is frimbly-central.*

Then he heard the door creak open behind him.

He whipped round to see a figure in the doorway: a tall, stooping man in a long black robe, his hood hanging low over his face.

I don't believe it! Jack thought. *Another hooded man!* 'You nearly made me jump out of my skin, mate!' he laughed, glad to see a real live human being after all the bats and spiders and white marble women. 'You're a bit lost if you're on your way to History Wee—'

But his words froze on his tongue as the man's hood slid back.

Those eyes were the scariest things Jack had ever seen.

Fifteen

A Sticky Situation

Emily and her mum had finished spinning. Now they'd moved on to demonstrating how to dye cloth using ancient plant dyes. Emily was up to her elbows in an iron pot of liquid made purple with elderberries and dandelion roots, when she heard a sound from outside the back of the tent.

'*Psst!*'

The voice seemed to come from just behind Emily's feet.

123

'It's me! I've got something.'

'Scott?' Emily turned to see a little flap of canvas hitching up from the grass. Scott was whispering through the gap. She glanced around the tent. Mum was busy showing a group of Saxon ladies how to grind sorrel roots. *Workers are entitled to take a break*, Emily told herself. *I'm sure there's something about it in the European Court of Human Rights. And, anyway, this cloth could do with being left to steep in the dye for a while.*

She lay flat and rolled out under the canvas.

Drift squeezed through after her.

Scott grinned down at them. 'Come on!' he said. 'I've got a sudden urge to buy a fishing rod!'

~

Ten minutes later, Scott, Emily and Drift were standing outside Brendan's Tackle and Bait on Pilchard Lane, a cobbled alley that ran from the high street to the seafront. The tiny shop window was a hotchpotch of fishing rods, reels and nets. Flamingo-pink cardboard stars advertised two-for-one deals on tubs of live maggots.

Scott had explained to Emily on the way that the Nancarrow family had owned the shop for generations, before they'd sold up and emigrated to Australia. 'With a bit of luck, the Nancarrow pattern could still be somewhere in the building,' he said. 'Let's go in. You can have a snoop around while I pretend to be looking at fishing rods.'

As they opened the door they were greeted with the chime of a bell and a pungent blast of maggot, worm and fish smells. Drift trotted in after Scott and Emily, sniffing the air in delight, like a wine expert sampling a glass of vintage claret.

'Can I help you there at all?' a tall, skinny man called out in an Irish accent. He was sitting behind the counter rearranging the penknives under the glass and listening to a play on the radio. Emily recognized Brendan Keenan, the owner.

'Er, yeah, I'm after a fishing rod,' Scott said.

'Well, you've come to the right place!'

While Scott and Brendan discussed the benefits of spincast versus spinning reels, Emily conducted a reconnaissance tour. The shop was jam-packed with fishing tackle, wading boots and barrels of maggots. The walls were lined with framed photos of people proudly holding up the record-breaking fish they'd caught. Oddly, there was a huge stag's head on the wall behind the counter.

Brendan looked up as he handed Scott a reel to try out. 'You're admiring old Percy there, I see,' he said to Emily.

'Percy?' Emily echoed.

Brendan laughed. 'That's what we've always called him. He was left up there by some previous owners way back when. He's hundreds of years old. Fine set of antlers, eh?'

But it wasn't Percy's antlers that had caught Emily's attention. It was a small pattern carved into the wooden plaque he was mounted on. She elbowed Scott in the ribs. 'Keep talking,' she muttered out of the side of her mouth.

'Could I have a look at those rods in the window?' Scott asked. 'The ones right in the corner.'

'Of course!' Brendan rubbed his hands together. 'I'll fetch them all out for you and you can take a good look.'

While Brendan was in the shop window, Emily ran round to the back of the counter and climbed the stepladder that was there for reaching bait down from the highest shelves. It wasn't easy in her long dress and cloak but soon she was looking Percy in the eye. He gazed back with a disapproving stare. She took her phone from her bag, snapped a photo of the pattern and scuttled back down the ladder.

Meanwhile, Scott felt so guilty about getting Brendan to show him every fishing rod in the shop that he agreed to buy one. 'I've only got ten pounds with me,' he said. 'I'll come back with the rest of the money later.'

Brendan smiled. 'No problem at all!'

This investigation was turning out to be pricey, Scott thought. He'd used up all his phone credit and now he was blowing half his savings on a fishing rod. He didn't even like fishing! Oh well, at least their mission had been a success. He could tell by the ear-to-ear grin on Emily's face that Percy had come up with the goods.

'Another Celtic knot pattern,' she said, high-fiving with Scott as soon as they'd left the shop. 'We'll have to check it against the tapestry in the secret room but I'm sure it's the Nancarrow pattern. Five down, one to go!'

Scott frowned. 'I can't believe that the one piece of the puzzle that's still missing is the Carter pattern!' He looked at his watch. 'Talking of being missing, I wonder where Jack's got to.'

—

Jack was rooted to the spot in Pendragon Chapel, mesmerized by those menacing eyes.

One black as night, Old Bob had said. *The other milky white like the skin on a rice pudding.*

Right now, both of those eyes were boring into Jack like twin laser beams.

The rest of the man's face wasn't going to win him any beauty contests either, Jack thought: bulging forehead, hooked nose, thin twisted lips. And now he'd also produced a sword from under his robe and was running his thumb along the blade as if testing it for sharpness. Jack wondered whether it was real, or a fake one for History Week. He didn't really want to find out.

'Er, can I help you?' he stammered.

'Yes, I rather think you can.' The hooded man's voice

was smooth, oily and dangerous, the way a cobra would sound if cobras could talk. 'You and your friends seem to know rather a lot about the Keepers of the Key.'

'Not really,' Jack mumbled. 'Hardly anything, actually.'

'Oh, no! Don't be so modest. I've been observing you. I know you have Josiah Lugg's notebook. And I know you've found most of the pieces of the key. Your girlfriend has it all written down in that pretty blue notebook of hers.'

'She's *not* my girlfriend,' Jack blurted, as if it made any difference. Being mistaken for an item with Emily was the least of his problems!

'Where is she?' The hooded man's black eye scanned the chapel. His white eye didn't move. 'And where's your brother?'

Jack shrugged. 'They're not here.'

The hooded man smiled a cold reptilian smile and stepped closer. Jack backed away but he was cornered against the marble woman on the tomb. Her elbow was digging into his back. And now Hood Features was so close Jack could feel his breath on his face. 'I need those notebooks!'

'Why?' Jack asked.

'You really don't know what you're dealing with, do you?' the hooded man spat. 'The Keepers were entrusted to guard the secret location of the Holy Grail. I have been searching for the Grail for many years. He who drinks from the Grail is granted eternal life. I will be immortal!'

Bonkers, more like! Jack thought. *Bonkers and armed with a sword.* It wasn't a good combination.

Suddenly the hooded man grabbed Jack's arm. 'Where's your phone?' he hissed. Spittle sprayed Jack's forehead. He didn't dare wipe it off. Instead he took one look at the sword and extracted his phone from his pocket.

'Call your brother! Tell him and the girl to meet you here. And to bring the notebooks with them. Make it sound normal. Don't let on there's anyone with you.' The hooded man raised the sword to his eyes and squinted along the blade. 'No funny business, do you understand?'

Jack gulped and nodded.

Scott and Emily had looked for Jack everywhere. He wasn't at any of the History Week events or eating doughnuts at Dotty's Tea Rooms or buying sweets at the newsagent. And he wasn't answering his phone.

'He's probably sulking at home because I wouldn't let him talk to Mrs Loveday,' Scott said.

But when they got back to Stone Cottage, Jack was nowhere to be seen.

Nor was his bike.

Scott groaned. 'Uh-oh! I hope he hasn't gone off on one of his mad solo missions.'

They were sitting in the living room wondering where to look next when Scott's phone rang.

'Hello there!' Jack's voice was suspiciously chirpy.

'What's up?' Scott asked. 'Don't tell me you need us to come and get you out of a sticky situation as usual!'

'Of course not! Nothing sticky going on at all.'

Scott shrugged at Emily and switched his phone to speaker. 'So where are you?' he asked. 'We've been looking everywhere.'

'I'm at Pendragon Chapel,' Jack said. 'You know, where we came that time during Operation Skeleton. I've found a clue.'

'What sort of a clue?'

'A really *super* one. I was in the library reading, as usual, and I found something that led me to the chapel.'

'Are you feeling alright in the head?' Scott asked.

'Oh, yes! Never felt better. Thing is, I need to check something, so can you come here quickly? And tell Em to bring her notebook with her.'

'Have you ever known Em *not* bring her notebook with her?'

'Oh, yes, I forgot. And bring Josiah Lugg's notebook too. Just get here soon.'

'Alright, keep your hair on,' Scott said. 'We'll be there soon.'

'Smashing!' Jack replied.

Scott kept staring at his phone after he'd hung up.

'*Smashing?*' he repeated. 'Since when did Jack use the word *smashing*?'

Emily nodded slowly. 'Or *super*. And it wasn't Operation Skeleton when we went to Pendragon Chapel, it was Operation Compass. And he knows I always have my notebook with me!'

'And why did he say he was in the library *as usual*?' Scott added. 'He never goes to the library if he can help it.'

There was a long silence.

Emily was the first to speak. 'Jack was trying to tell us something.'

'He's in trouble,' Scott said. '*Big trouble!*'

Sixteen

Rescue Plan

Emily and Scott sat at either end of the sofa staring at each other in dismay. 'Someone must have taken Jack hostage. They've forced him to phone and tell us to bring the notebooks,' Scott said eventually. 'It sounds like they're trying to find out what we know about the Keepers of the Key . . .'

'I should've trusted my investigator's instinct all along,' Emily murmured.

'*Instinct?* What do you mean?'

'I kept getting this weird feeling we were being followed. It started when I was up in the tower at St Michael's. I thought I saw a hooded figure by the church gate. But when I looked again it had gone.'

Scott gulped. 'That's strange. I felt it too. Like someone walked behind us in the graveyard. But I didn't see anyone.'

'Maybe it's Harry Mabbutt, the clock-winder,' Emily said. 'He was at the church. He could have heard us talking about Josiah Lugg's notebook and the Keepers and now he's got hold of Jack to try to find out more.'

But Scott shook his head. 'Mabbutt came down from winding the clock *after* you'd come down from the tower. That can't be who you saw.' He raked his hair off his face and clutched his temples. 'And, anyway, I saw a man at West Rock Beach, too – just after those timbers nearly fell on me. It looked like a monk walking along the sand. He was much too tall to be Harry.'

'Why didn't you say anything?' Emily asked.

'I thought it was just one of the History Week people.'

Emily thought for a moment. 'It could have been Colin Warnock. He was wearing monk's robes.'

'No, Colin's robes were brown. This guy had black robes. And a black hood.'

Emily stared down at her hands, which were still stained bright purple from the elderberry and dandelion root mixture. Scott chewed his thumbnail. Neither of them wanted to admit it, but they both knew the truth. It was Scott who finally said it out loud. 'This is Old Bob's hooded man, isn't it?'

Emily nodded slowly. 'He bashed Old Bob on the head just after he said he was going to tell us the second verse of the *Keepers of the Key* rhyme. The Hood obviously didn't want us to get that information. He wants to find the secret location before we do.'

Scott shuddered. 'He's dangerous. And now he's holding Jack at Pendragon Chapel until we hand over everything we know.' He jumped up from the sofa. 'Come on, let's get moving. We have to rescue Jack.'

Emily stuffed the notebooks into her bag, called Drift and ran after Scott. But as they wheeled their bikes out into the lane, something was bothering her. 'How did the Hood find out we were investigating the Keepers of the Key in the first place? We didn't tell anyone.'

Scott stopped and looked down at his shoes. 'I think it may have been my fault!' he said in a small voice.

Emily's eyes widened with surprise. 'How?'

'I went on an Arthurian Legends website and asked if anyone knew about the Keepers of the Key,' Scott told Emily as they got on their bikes. 'I didn't give anything away about what we'd found out. Honest! I just asked. Anyway, I only had one response. It was from someone called Sangreal, saying he would help if I sent a private message telling him what I knew. It sounded like the guy was just fishing for information so I ignored him. I thought that was the end of it.'

Emily was about to berate Scott for ignoring her warning about secrecy, but she could see that he felt bad enough already. And, anyway, there was no time. They had to get to Pendragon Chapel as fast as they could. 'So you think this Sangreal could be the Hood?' she asked as they set off along Church Lane, heads down against the driving rain.

'I'm sure of it,' Scott replied. He didn't mention that Sangreal had sent a second message: *Knowledge can be dangerous.* Scott had taken no notice, thinking it was just someone's idea of a joke. It didn't seem funny now. Nor did the fact that he'd used the name Mad Jack. Guilt twisted like a knife blade between his ribs. His brother might be the most annoying person on the planet, but Scott would never forgive himself if anything happened to him.

Suddenly Emily jammed on her brakes. 'Hang on! Are we sure it's a good idea to hand over everything we know to this lunatic?'

Scott kept pedalling. 'We'll have to!' he shouted over his shoulder. 'It's the only way we'll get Jack back.'

Emily raced after him. 'Think about it. This Sangreal guy is so desperate to get his hands on whatever the Keepers were guarding that he was prepared to hit Old Bob on the head and to kidnap Jack. It must be really important . . . it could be dangerous in the wrong hands.'

'You're not saying you believe all that rubbish about

the Holy Grail?' Scott asked, banking sharply as he took the bend onto the coast road at high speed.

Emily was right behind him. 'I don't know. I just don't think we should lead a madman to it.'

'What do you suggest? We just let Jack take his chances?'

'Of course not!' Emily shouted. 'I've got a plan.'

—

As they cycled, Emily panted out her rescue plan. 'I go to the chapel with the notebooks and pretend I'm going to hand them over. I'll keep the Hood talking as long as I can. Meanwhile, you sneak into the manor and go through that secret tunnel we found during Operation Compass – the one that starts behind the fireplace in the kitchen and comes out . . .'

'. . . through the side of the Pendragon tomb in the chapel!' Scott exclaimed, finishing her sentence.

'Exactly. So you creep out and ambush the Hood from behind. Then Jack and I join the attack and help pin him down.'

Scott had to admit it was a good plan. And he certainly didn't have a better one. He gave a grim nod. 'OK. Let's do it.'

—

Scott stood outside the back door of Pendragon Manor. He'd said goodbye to Emily and Drift at the edge of

137

the grounds and they'd headed off through the woods towards the chapel. Now all Scott had to do was sneak into the house, across the kitchen and round the back of the fireplace. Easier said than done! The kitchen was usually buzzing with cooks preparing meals for conferences and events. They might just notice a guy wandering past and climbing into the fireplace! But he had to give it a go, so as soon as the coast was clear he slipped inside, hurried along the corridor and peeped in through the open kitchen door.

There were three cooks at work, all dressed in white caps and aprons. One was chopping onions, one whisking cream and one rolling pastry. A man in a chef's hat stood at the stove tasting something from a saucepan. The radio was blaring Jessie J into the steamy air.

Scott looked around. He needed a distraction. He was considering the old standby of setting off a fire alarm when he noticed, just next to the door, a massive multi-storey metal trolley laden with trays of dirty dishes.

The trolley was on wheels.

'Sorry about this,' Scott muttered under his breath as he gave it a hefty shove. The trolley hurtled across the floor and slammed into a table with an ear-crunching crash. An explosion of plates and bowls clattered and smashed in all directions.

The cooks and the chef all raced to the scene of the crockery volcano.

At the same time, Scott ran to the huge brick fireplace at the other end of the kitchen and pushed open the small metal door at the back. Just before he dived through, he pressed SEND on the text he'd prepared for Emily: *in tunnel now.* He would have no signal once he was undergound, and this was the only way he could let her know when to begin her part of the operation.

Scott switched on his torch and began to jog along the tunnel.

He hadn't gone far when he noticed the torch beam was starting to fade.

—

Meanwhile, Emily was waiting in the undergrowth near Pendragon Chapel. She jumped when her phone buzzed with the message from Scott.

'Good. It should take him about ten minutes to get through the tunnel,' she whispered to Drift. She waited ten, then gave it an extra minute for good measure. She didn't want to have to keep the Hood talking for too long. He'd soon get suspicious if he thought she was playing for time. 'Come on Drift, we're going in!'

Emily marched up to the chapel door and pushed it open.

Seventeen

Better Late than Never

Emily peered into the gloom. Through the swathes of cobwebs she saw Jack lying beside the Pendragon tomb. He was tied up as if wrapped in silken threads by an enormous spider. A gag had been bound round his mouth.

A tall hooded man in long black robes glided towards Emily from the other end of the chapel. 'Ah, good, the girl!' he said. 'Where's the other boy?'

'Scott couldn't come,' Emily replied, hoping she sounded braver than she felt. The man looked down his crooked nose at her. She made the mistake of trying to hold his gaze. The unearthly eyes made her feel cold to her bones. At her side Drift growled softly. Emily gulped and looked at the man's cleft chin instead. 'He had to help out at History Week,' she said.

The Hood blinked slowly. 'Did you bring the notebooks?'

Emily nodded.

'Give them to me!'

'No way! Let Jack go first!'

The Hood let out a bloodless laugh. 'Do you think I'd be so foolish? If I let him go you'll just take the books and run off. I can't let that happen. You kids have dabbled in ancient secrets you do not understand. Now *give me the notebooks*!'

Emily clasped her bag to her side. 'Not until you let Jack go!'

The Hood shook his head and stepped closer. He held out his bony hands. The sleeves of his robe hung down from arms as thin as sticks. Emily noticed that a small triangle of black cloth had been torn from one sleeve. Instantly, she remembered the fabric snagged on the nail at the shepherd's hut. *That proved it!* The Hood had been following them. He'd been in the hut while they were down in the fuggy hole! He must have positioned those timbers to fall on them when they came back up.

Emily's legs felt as weak and wobbly as wet tissue paper. The guy was clearly crazy. And he'd stop at nothing to get hold of their information about the Keepers of the Key. She glanced towards the Pendragon tomb. *Where was Scott?* It must be at least twenty minutes since he'd sent the text. What if something had happened in the tunnel and he wasn't coming? She didn't allow herself to think about what that would mean. Instead she took a deep breath.

'You could let Jack come to the door but with his feet still tied,' she said. 'That way he can't run away. Then I'll give you the notebooks.'

The Hood sneered. 'I don't think so!'

Emily was wondering how much longer it would be before the Hood got fed up with bargaining and made a grab for the notebooks – and for her – when she heard a scraping sound. *It had to be Scott!* She forced herself not to look at the Pendragon tomb again and give him away. But now there was another problem! The Hood had walked back further into the chapel and was now standing over Jack, right next to the tomb. If Scott slid open the hidden door in the side, he'd be seen straight away.

Heart pounding, Emily stepped backwards through the open door behind her and placed the notebooks – her beautiful blue and silver one and Josiah Lugg's brown leather one – side by side on the ground just outside the chapel. 'OK. I give up,' she said loudly. 'I just want to get my friend back. You can have the books.'

Overcome by greed, the Hood lunged towards Emily, fell to his knees on the doorstep and reached out, one claw-like hand groping for each of the books.

At the same moment, Scott sprang out from the tomb and leaped onto his back.

The Hood was stronger than he looked. He pulled away and twisted round, his hands reaching for Scott's throat.

Scott raised the brass candlestick he'd grabbed from the end of the tomb. He was about to take a swipe at the Hood when Drift pounced. With a ferocious snarl, the valiant dog snatched a fold of black robe between his teeth and tugged with all his strength.

The Hood roared a curse as he toppled over backwards.

The back of his head hit the solid stone doorstep with a dull *thunk*.

He tried to get up, gave a whimper and then lay back again. Slowly, almost-transparent eyelids threaded with a tracery of blue veins closed over his terrible eyes.

Scott stood over the man like a statue, still holding the candlestick aloft. 'But I didn't touch him!' he stammered. 'Have . . . have we *killed* him?'

Emily knelt and checked. 'No, he's breathing. He's just knocked himself out.'

Scott almost keeled over with relief. He let go of the candlestick. It clattered onto the doorstep and rolled away into the brambles.

Emily looked up at him and grinned. 'Good work! But what took you so long?'

'Sorry, the torch battery died. I had a spare but it took a few minutes to change them over in the dark.'

Emily laughed. 'Oh, well, better late than never!' She gave Drift a hug. 'And that was a brilliant pounce!'

Drift wagged his tail.

'Oompphhh! Ooommmpph!'

Emily and Scott looked back into the chapel to see Jack wriggling towards them like a giant caterpillar.

Scott ran and pulled off the gag and began untying the ropes.

'Cheers!' Jack said, rubbing his sore wrists. 'You want to watch that bloke. He's a total fruit loop!'

'We had noticed!' Scott laughed.

'Quick, he's coming round,' Emily shouted. 'Bring those ropes over!'

The Hood was sitting up and trying to lash out but, between the three of them, the friends soon had him trussed up like a parcel.

'Now what?' Jack asked.

Scott leaned against the stone arch of the doorframe. Now the adrenaline burst was over, he suddenly felt exhausted. 'Now I call the police and tell them we've caught Old Bob's attacker for them.'

Next morning Aunt Kate insisted that Jack have a quiet day at home after his hostage ordeal. Jack was making the most of it. He snuggled under a blanket on the sofa with Boomerang, watching an old Doctor Who episode, a steady supply of cake and hot chocolate within easy reach.

'Keep the noise down!' he told Scott and Emily, who were sitting at the table working on the investigation. 'I've got post-traumatic stress, you know.'

'As if!' Scott snorted. 'I still can't see why you had to go charging off to Pendragon Chapel on your own in the first place.'

Jack explained, yet again, how he'd gone to the library and discovered that King Arthur's father was called Uther Pendragon. 'So I figured I'd find the Holy Grail in the old Pendragon Chapel by myself. *Pendragon.* The clue's in the name!'

'But you didn't find it,' Scott pointed out bluntly.

Jack's face fell. Then he grinned. 'True, but if I hadn't lured Old Hood Features to the chapel and heroically let myself be taken hostage, we wouldn't have caught him. And Old Bob's attacker would still be on the loose!'

Scott shook his head at Jack's creative version of events. But at least one part of it was true: the police had arrested the Hood at the chapel. Detective Inspector Hassan had called earlier to let them know that Old Bob had officially identified the man as his attacker.

The hooded man – whose real name was Stewart Gibbs – was now in a cell at Carrickstowe Police Station until a date for his court case could be arranged.

'And another thing,' Jack said, selecting the biggest piece from the plate of chocolate cake. 'I've been right about the King Arthur connection all along! The Keepers of the Key *were* guarding the Holy Grail. Hood Features told me all about it while I let him tie me up.'

'Hmm,' Scott murmured. 'Like we believe *everything* that nutcase says!'

But Emily agreed with Jack. 'The Keepers were obviously guarding something really important. And I looked up the username Stewart Gibbs was using to talk to you on that Arthurian Legends website. *Sangreal* means Holy Grail!'

Scott sniffed. 'So he picked a fancy user name! That doesn't mean anything.'

Jack stretched lazily. 'Well, *whatever* this top-secret gizmo is, at least now Hood Features is locked up we don't have to worry about him getting his mitts on it before we do.'

Emily looked up from her notebook. 'Exactly! We can take our time solving the puzzle of the patterns and Lugg's Bible codes and everything. What we need is a really good brainstorm.' She spread out her notes and papers on the table.

Jack groaned, wondering whether she was going to

produce a flipchart and a PowerPoint presentation as well.

'Now,' she said. 'We're pretty sure from the second verse of Old Bob's rhyme that the secret object is hidden somewhere in the castle. *He who would be king, With all the king's power, Six turns must make, From the dungeon to the tower,*' she recited.

'So far so good,' Jack agreed. 'Dungeons and towers. That's your basic castle scenario.'

Scott nodded. 'And we think that, somehow, the six pattern pieces that the Keepers were guarding all fit together to make a "key" to open the secret hiding place. And then there's Josiah Lugg's notebook.' He reached for the book and opened it at the back page. '*Read between the lines, six turns to find ...*'

'It's *six turns* again! The same as Old Bob's verse,' Jack grumbled. 'What are these mysterious *turns* they keep going on about?'

Emily frowned. '*Read between the lines* means you have to look for a hidden meaning. I think Lugg's trying to tell us that we have to work out those six Bible codes to find out *where* in the castle the six *turns* are hidden. But that still doesn't tell us *what* they are.'

'Hmm, that's the question,' Scott murmured, as he picked up the paper with Jack's rubbing of the Goff pattern from the fireplace, and rotated it to examine it from a different angle.

Jack stared at him for a moment. 'Turns!' he cried

suddenly. 'Lugg's talking about the patterns! We have to find the patterns in the castle and *turn* them so they line up in some way.'

Emily beamed at Jack. 'Genius! I told you brainstorming would work.'

Scott nodded, even though he hated to admit Jack was on to something. 'Yes, that could be it. The six patterns that match these' – he pointed at the print-outs on the table – 'could be engraved into tiles or stones or something that can be rotated. I guess they're linked up to some kind of hidden locking mechanism inside the walls, so that when they're all turned in the right way to make the pattern pieces fit together, the secret hiding place will spring open . . .'

'So we leg it up to the castle,' Jack said, 'and start turning things, and – *ker-ching!* – we find the Holy Grail!'

Emily frowned. 'Not so fast! We've got to work out those Bible codes first and we're still missing the sixth pattern, the *Carter* pattern. Think! Where could it be?' She glanced at the TV in the corner, which was now showing the local morning news. 'I can't focus with that noise. Jack, can you turn it off?'

Jack's hand was poised over the Off switch (there was no remote control for Aunt Kate's old black and white telly!) when Emily shouted, 'No! Leave it on!'

'Make your mind up!' Jack grumbled.

'Shh!' Emily hissed. 'They're saying something about Castle Key.'

They all fell silent and watched.

'And finally,' the newsreader announced, 'organizers of the famous Castle Key History Week have run into problems. While carrying out a safety inspection at Key Castle, ahead of the battle re-enactment to be held there tomorrow, major safety issues were discovered.'

An image of the ruins of Key Castle came up on the screen.

'It appears,' the newsreader went on, 'that the cliffs beneath the castle are crumbling away much faster than was previously thought. Parts of the ruins are in danger of slipping into the sea. Engineers have given permission for the battle re-enactment to go ahead tomorrow but, immediately after the battle ends at midday, the castle will be closed to all members of the public for at least three months while work is carried out to make it safe.'

The newsreader shuffled her papers and moved on to the weather.

'Three months!' Emily gasped. 'We can't wait that long to find the Holy Grail!'

Eighteen

Read Between the Lines

Jack switched off the TV.

Emily looked at the boys in dismay. 'The castle's going to be closed for three months! Tomorrow morning's our last chance to search for the Holy Grail. So much for taking our time!'

'But Jack and I are signed up for the battle re-enactment tomorrow!' Scott pointed out. 'We'll be busy fighting off the Saxon invasion.'

'You'll just have to sneak away for a while.' Emily had never thought she'd be *pleased* that girls weren't allowed to take part in the fighting – in fact, she'd been planning to dress up as a boy again and join in – but now it was a bonus! She'd be with all the other women and girls, preparing food and tending to the injured warriors. It would be easy to make up an excuse and slip away into the castle.

Scott threw himself down on the sofa. 'Aren't you forgetting a few minor details? Like, we don't have all the pattern pieces, we don't know how they fit together and we don't know where to find them in the castle.'

Emily checked her watch. 'It's ten twenty-three now. That gives us twenty-five hours and thirty-seven minutes till the castle closes at midday tomorrow . . .'

Jack laughed. 'So no pressure then!'

Scott sighed and got up from the sofa. 'OK. I guess it's worth a try. Let's start by seeing if we can work out how these patterns fit together, even if there's one missing.'

'I'll get some more cake,' Jack said. 'We're going to need it.'

Emily laid the five Celtic knot patterns out on the table. The first three were print-outs of photos: the pattern painted on the Trevithick fishing boats, the one carved on the White family headstones and the Nancarrow pattern from Percy the stag's plaque in the fishing tackle shop. Then there was Jack's wax crayon rubbing of the Goff pattern on the hearth, and finally the page that had fallen out of Josiah Lugg's notebook with the small pattern drawn in the corner.

Scott started to shuffle the pieces of paper around. 'It would be easier if they were all the same size.'

'What you need is a Sketch-a-Graph.'

The voice belonged to Aunt Kate, who had just come in to check on Jack.

'A *What*-a-graph?' Jack asked.

Aunt Kate smiled and looked over her glasses. 'I heard Scott say you want to make all those patterns the same size. The Sketch-a-Graph is an old toy that was designed to make a larger or smaller copy of a drawing. Your dad and Uncle Leo used to have one. They played with it for ages on rainy days.'

'Those dudes knew how to have a good time!' Scott said sarcastically, wondering, not for the first time, how anyone had actually survived before computer games were invented.

'I think it's still up in that old toy box in your room,' Aunt Kate said.

Scott rolled his eyes at no one in particular as he trudged up the stairs to look for it. No doubt this Sketch-a-Graph would be rubbish. In fact, he was sure this whole enterprise was doomed to failure. How on earth were they going to crack a secret that'd been lost hundreds of years ago by lunchtime tomorrow?

The old toy box was a large battered wooden chest that stood in the corner of the boys' attic bedroom. Generations of Carter kids had gouged their names in it with compass points and plastered it with stickers. Scott and Jack had taken a quick look inside when they first came to Stone Cottage. Unimpressed by the collection of tin soldiers and marbles, they now just used the old box as an extra surface on which to dump their stuff.

Scott swept a heap of discarded clothes onto the floor, unlocked the box with the little metal key and lifted the lid. The soldiers and marbles were still there, along with model aeroplane kits, a headless Action Man and a cowboy hat. He dug down and found a cardboard box marked *Sketch-a-Graph*. On the lid a rosy-cheeked boy was grinning insanely as he enlarged a drawing of a cartoon puppy.

Scott let go of the lid of the toy box. As it slammed shut, a faded *Star Wars* sticker detached itself from near the lock and fluttered to the floor. Scott glanced at the patch of lighter-coloured wood it had left behind.

He did a double take.

Were those faint squiggly lines what he thought they were?

He looked closer.

A small Celtic knot pattern had been engraved on the wooden chest.

'Did you find the Sketch-a-Graph?' Emily asked Scott as he came back into the living room.

Scott held up the box.

'What's up with you?' Jack laughed. 'You've got a grin on your face nearly as daft as the one on that kid on the lid!'

'I found something else,' Scott said. 'Come and see.'

Mystified, Jack and Emily followed Scott upstairs.

'Ta-da!' Scott crowed, pointing at the toy box. 'The Carter pattern! It was here all the time, right under our noses!'

Jack stared in amazement for a moment, and then laughed. 'Of course! This box came from the Carter side of the family. Aunt Kate told me ages ago that Granny and Granddad had left it here so Dad and Uncle Leo would have some stuff to play with when they came back every holiday.' He looked at the box with a newfound respect. The wood was worn smooth with age. The hinges and lock were fashioned from solid brass. 'I bet it was once a sea chest, used for stowing smuggled loot by generations of smuggling Carters . . .'

Scott and Emily weren't listening. They were too busy photographing the pattern and printing it out on Aunt Kate's old inkjet printer.

Soon the three friends were gathered round the table

in the living room again, assembling the Sketch-a-Graph.

The contraption was made up of a lattice of hinged plastic struts that could be extended or pushed close together. A pencil was slotted into a holder at one end, and used to trace over the picture to be copied. As it moved, another pencil at the other end of the device automatically drew the same design on a piece of paper positioned beneath it. The size of the copy depended on how far you opened out the lattice. At least, that was the theory! It took a few false starts, and some very cross words, but eventually they got the hang of it. Soon they had a copy of each of the six patterns – all exactly the same size.

Emily carefully cut round each one to produce six tile-sized squares of paper. 'Now, we've just got to fit them together.'

'Easy-peasy!' Jack said. He put two of the squares side by side. The lines of the knot patterns all connected. He grabbed another piece but, whichever way he turned it, the lines wouldn't match up. He turned the first piece round. Now the third one worked but the second was wrong. He shuffled the squares like playing cards and tried again. It was even worse this time. Instead of a neat symmetrical knot, he'd produced a tangled mess. He threw the pieces down. 'It's impossible!'

'No it's not,' Scott said, pushing his floppy fringe back out of his eyes and frowning at the paper squares.

'They could go in two rows of three or one row of six or a cross or a triangle or a Z-shape . . .' he muttered to himself, '. . . and the pieces could be in any order within those arrangements. We just have to try all the permutations.'

Jack and Emily exchanged glances. 'Yes, of course! *Permutations!*' Jack said, nodding sagely, as if he had any idea what a permutation was. 'I think we should leave Scott to work it out in peace.'

'Good idea,' Emily agreed. 'We'll get on with figuring out what those Bible verses in Josiah Lugg's notebook mean.'

Jack had been thinking more along the lines of retiring to the sofa for a power nap. He sighed as Emily waved a page of Lugg's notebook under his nose. The writing was all over the place: words were scribbled backwards, upside-down, on top of each other. 'This is worse than my geography homework,' he joked.

'Lugg only had a few weeks left to live when he wrote this,' Emily explained. 'I think he was delirious. But if you look closely, you can see the numbers of the six Bible verses. I've looked them all up and copied them out.' Emily slid her own notebook across the table to Jack. Six Bible verses were written out in her neat handwriting. 'If our theory is right, these tell us where in the castle to find the patterns that we have to turn.'

Jack shook his head as he read the verses. 'But none

of these has anything to do with finding patterns in castles!'

Emily sighed impatiently. 'That's because the information is in some kind of secret code to stop the dark forces getting hold of it. That's why Lugg said *read between the lines*. We have to use every third letter or every tenth word or something.' She chewed her pen. 'Problem is, I've tried everything I can think of and nothing works.'

Jack shrugged. It was just like Emily to make things more complicated than necessary. 'Maybe old Luggo wasn't using secret codes, but was just saying that he *literally* wrote something in between the lines of print in the Bible . . .'

Emily rolled her eyes. 'That's way too obvious! And anyway,' she added, 'how would that even work? There are billions of Bibles on the planet. How would we know which one he'd written in?'

Scott looked up from rearranging the pattern squares. 'You could start by looking in that great big one on the lectern in St Michael's. That'd be the obvious one for the priest there to have used.'

Jack glowered at his brother. 'I was just about to say that!'

Emily laid her silver pen carefully on the table. 'I suppose it *might* be worth a look.'

Within minutes, Emily, Jack and Drift were hurtling into the church. Luckily it was empty. They headed straight for the lectern at the front, which was in the shape of a mighty eagle sculpted from gleaming brass, holding up the Bible on its outstretched wings.

'What's the first verse on the list?' Jack asked.

Emily consulted her notebook. 'Daniel Three, Thirteen.'

Jack turned over the pages until he found the Book of Daniel near the end of the Old Testament. Carefully he turned to Chapter Three, Verse Thirteen. 'Here it is,' he said, peering at the tiny text.

Emily was so excited she practically elbowed Jack out of the way. 'Is there anything there?'

Nineteen

Breakthrough!

J ack and Emily stood at the lectern and stared at the
white space between the lines of the Bible verse.

Emily took her torch and magnifying glass from her
bag but, even with bright light and magnification, there
were no messages to be seen.

They tried the next verse and the next.

Nothing!

Jack could hardly believe his brilliant brainwave had

failed. This was the end of the line. If they couldn't figure out Lugg's clues, there was no way they'd be able to find the patterns in the castle tomorrow. He began to traipse back down the aisle. But when he realized Emily wasn't following, he turned back.

She had her nose pressed to the Bible.

'Er, what exactly are you doing?' Jack asked.

Emily looked up and grinned. 'I can smell lemon juice.'

Jack made a blank face. Had his friend completely lost the plot?

'You can use lemon juice to make invisible ink,' Emily explained. 'That's how Lugg has written between the lines!'

'Uh-uh!' Jack snorted. 'We're talking about 1755. Even Drift wouldn't be able to smell two-hundred-and-fifty-year-old lemon juice!'

Sitting patiently at Emily's side, Drift pricked up his ears at his name.

'Come and try for yourself,' Emily said.

Jack went back and sniffed the old paper. He almost choked as a powerful lemony whiff shot up his nostrils. He shook his head. 'That's the brass polish Mrs Loveday uses on the eagle,' he said. 'Aunt Kate uses the same stuff.'

Emily looked so disappointed Jack thought she might burst into tears.

'Well, it might still be worth a try,' he said, just to cheer her up.

Emily's face brightened. 'Lemon juice turns brown when you heat it. Quick, get a candle!'

Jack was horrified. 'You can't start wafting candle flames around the Bible. What if it gets burnt?'

Emily chewed the inside of her cheek. 'Oh, yeah, good point. We'll use my torch instead. The bulb gets really hot.'

Emily held the torch beneath the page. A minute passed, then two, then five.

Jack stared so hard his eyes were watering. This was crazy. There was no invisible ink, just Fresh Lemon Sparkle Brass Polish. He blinked. Then he saw it! A ghostly beige line was appearing in the margin. And then a faint loop, a dot and another line – now he could see a letter, two letters, a whole word, a sentence!

Emily was so excited she wrapped Jack in a bear hug.

Jack was so stoked he hugged her back!

Then he realized what he was doing. He jumped back and read out the secret message: '*Easier by far to enter than to leave*. What's that supposed to mean?'

Emily shrugged. 'I don't know. Let's find the next one. People will start arriving for the morning service soon.'

Jack almost imploded with impatience as he waited for writing to emerge between the text of Luke, Chapter Eleven, Verse Forty-four. '*Where no living creature comes between the man and the heavens but for birds on the wing,*' he read at last.

As he turned to the third verse Jack wondered whether Josiah Lugg had been even crazier than the Hood. It seemed they'd solved the codes only to find riddles instead!

⸺

By the time Emily and Jack burst back into the living room of Stone Cottage, they had uncovered all six hidden messages.

And Scott had made a breakthrough too.

Jack and Emily stared down at the six squares of paper set out on the living-room table. The interweaving lines of each piece joined together to form a single flowing Celtic knot pattern.

'They line up in a single row of six,' Scott explained.

Emily beamed at him. 'That's brilliant! I knew you'd crack it!'

'It could be a column, not a row,' Jack pointed out, since he was looking at it from halfway round the table. 'Maybe it goes from top to bottom, not side to side.'

Suddenly Emily began jumping up and down on the spot. She pointed at the pieces on the table and waved her notebook. Then she pointed at the floor and then at the ceiling.

Scott and Jack shrugged at each other. 'It might be a new disco routine,' Scott laughed.

'Or she's got fleas,' Jack suggested.

Now Emily was making 'ooh ooh' noises, as if trying

to speak with a roast potato in her mouth.

At last Emily calmed down enough to talk. 'You're brilliant, too, Jack!' she panted. 'It *is* a column – but it goes from bottom to top, not top to bottom. The rhyme says you make six turns *from the dungeon to the tower*. So, you find the first pattern piece in the *dungeon* and you turn it into this position . . .' She pointed to the first of the squares.

Scott nodded. 'Right. I get it. Then you go up to the next floor, you find this piece,' he pointed to the second square, 'and turn it to this position.'

'Exactly,' Emily said. 'And you keep going until you've got all six pieces lined up like this, all the way up to the top floor.'

'Which is the *tower*!' Jack cried. Now he was the one dancing around the room. 'Of course! Those riddles of Lugg's tell you which room the pattern is in on each floor.' He grabbed Emily's notebook and read out the first message. '*Easier by far to enter than to leave.* That's the dungeon. It's easy to get in because the jailer throws you in, but then it's locked so it's not easy to get out.'

'Exactly,' Emily said. 'And this message about nothing between you and the heavens except for a bird could refer to the tower – because you're at the highest point of the castle with nobody above you.'

'OK,' Scott said. 'That makes sense. That's the dungeon and the tower, the two rooms we already knew about from Old Bob's rhyme. What about the other four in between?'

'Try this one,' Jack said, reading out the third hidden riddle. *'A man comes out with less than he went in but still feels better.'*

'Hmm . . . something that you want to get rid of?' Scott muttered. 'I don't know. Spots? Annoying younger brothers?'

'But you don't go to a particular room for that,' Emily pointed out. She ducked as Jack aimed a cushion across the table at Scott.

Scott was about to fire it back when he stopped mid-launch. 'Oh, I know! It's the toilet.'

Emily looked baffled. 'The toilet?'

Scott laughed. 'I'm really not going to explain it to you, Em!'

By the time they'd solved all the riddles it was dark. They had six different rooms, which they figured would each be on a different floor of the castle. Emily listed them in her notebook:

Dungeon
Kitchen
Great hall
Lady's bedchamber
Toilet
Tower

The three friends high-fived.

It had been a good day's work.

The Holy Grail was almost within their grasp!

—

The Battle of Castle Key commenced at nine o'clock sharp the following morning. The Cornish Britons took up position on the cliff top, crowding into the flat area around the castle ruins – although, of course, when the original battle took place in 722, the Norman stone castle had not yet been built. In those days Key Castle had been a wooden fort that protected the small Cornish settlement.

The rain had given way at last to bright sunshine. It glinted on the warriors' swords and spears and lit up the rainbow colours of fluttering banners and flags. This battle was the Grand Finale of History Week and the foot soldiers had been joined by knights on horseback and wooden chariots for the chieftains.

Armed with battle-axes and shields, their faces blue with war paint, Scott and Jack jostled near the moat with the other Britons, while Jago Merrick gave his troops their final battle orders. They were to hold the high ground against the invading Saxon armies who had swarmed across the narrow causeway from the mainland, breaching the island's defences, and were now mustering on North Moor.

Meanwhile, a second operation was in progress: one

that had also been planned with military precision. Scott, Jack and Emily were each equipped with a torch, a note of Lugg's six clues, a photocopy of the six pieces of the Celtic knot pattern in the correct sequence, and their mobile phones – all concealed beneath their cloaks to avoid detection by the eagle-eyed History Week organizers.

While the boys prepared for battle, Emily was busy in the outdoor kitchen near the museum – which was built onto the side of the castle ruins – peeling carrots for the huge pot of broth that was cooking over the fire, ready to feed the hungry warriors after a tough morning of seeing off the Saxons. Emily waited until everyone was busy then muttered something about needing to go to the bathroom.

She called Drift and headed for the museum entrance. The museum was closed to the public, but Emily knew it had been left unlocked because she'd seen Mrs Loveday go in earlier to fetch the first-aid kit when she'd cut her finger. She looked over her shoulder to make sure she wasn't being watched, then she and Drift slipped in through the door. They ran across the gift shop and through another door at the back into a long passageway that led past the museum offices.

Emily deliberately didn't notice the large sign that said this part of the castle was closed to the public for safety reasons.

She didn't stop running until she came to a steep,

narrow flight of stone steps. An arrow pointed downwards. Above it a sign said MUSEUM STORES – STAFF ONLY.

Emily had been exploring the castle ruins for years. She knew every nook and cranny. And she knew that the museum's storeroom had once been the old castle dungeons. She could feel cold, clammy air coming up from underground, as if the earth were breathing beneath her. It was inky dark down there too.

The dungeon! That was where the first piece of the pattern was hidden.

The plan was that Emily and Drift would start the search on their own. The boys would come and join in as soon as they could sneak away from the battle. Emily was secretly hoping to have found at least three of the patterns before the boys turned up.

But her hopes were dashed the moment she reached the bottom of the staircase and shone her torch on the heavy steel door in front of her. It wasn't the original dungeon door, of course. This one had been installed by the museum a few years ago to protect their valuable historical objects when they weren't out on display.

Which was why it was secured with a massive padlock and a security keypad!

Twenty

From the Dungeon to the Tower

Emily's heart sank.

She jiggled the handle but it was no good.

She leaned against the door to the dungeon and pressed her forehead against the ice-cold steel.

Furious, Emily kicked the wall.

She yelped as her big toe stubbed against the solid stone. Her soft leather boots offered no protection. She crouched down to rub her toe.

That's when she noticed that one of the stones low down in the wall near the doorframe was protruding from the rest. She took a closer look, blinking away the tears of frustration that were filling her eyes.

Suddenly, she was scrubbing the tears away and grabbing the photocopy of the Celtic knot patterns that she'd tucked into the belt of her long dress. She directed her torch onto the stone. Yes! It matched the first pattern in the sequence that Scott had worked out.

The only problem was that it was upside down. She needed to turn it by 180 degrees to match up with the next pattern in the sequence. Unsure how to move the stone, Emily poked and prodded at it. Just when she thought nothing would work, there was a soft click and it popped forwards a little as if on a spring. Now the small square stone turned easily in her hand. She rotated it to the correct position.

The first of the six turns was complete!

Emily and Drift raced back up the steps. They were hurrying along the corridor when Emily heard footsteps behind her.

An irritated voice was saying, 'I'm sure I heard someone!'

It was two of the History Week marshals, who were patrolling the castle to make sure people didn't stray into the closed-off areas! Emily couldn't risk being caught out of bounds. They'd escort her back to her carrot-peeling duties and she might not get another chance to slip away. She tried the handle of the first door she passed. It was open. She beckoned to Drift and they shot inside.

Emily leaned back against the door, heart thumping. She looked around. She was in an ordinary office with a desk, computer and bookshelves, but the room itself was clearly ancient, with rough stone walls and stone slabs beneath the modern rugs on the floor. A huge walk-in fireplace had been left exposed as a feature on one wall, along with metal hooks that must once have been used for hanging pots and pans above the flames. It seemed this room was part of the old kitchen.

Emily noticed a square hole in the wall to one side of the fireplace. The occupant of the office was using it as a handy spot for a potted fern. *It looks like a pizza oven*, Emily thought. *But that can't be right. Surely they didn't have pizza in mediaeval times ...*

Suddenly she realized she was on to something. It wasn't a pizza oven, it was a bread oven. And Josiah Lugg's next riddle was about bread. *The staff of life is made within these walls.* Scott had looked up the phrase *staff of life* on the internet and found that it meant bread, so they'd figured that Lugg was telling them to look in the kitchen – where bread was made. But, in fact, maybe he'd been more specific than that – bread was made within the *oven* walls, not just the kitchen walls.

Emily ran to the bread oven, pulled out the potted fern and shone her torch inside. On the back wall, a small soot-blackened stone bore the now-familiar traces of a Celtic knot pattern. She reached in, sending a spider scurrying from its web, pressed the stone and felt it turn under her hand.

'Yes!' she breathed to Drift. 'Two down, four to go!'

She texted the boys to tell them the news, then slipped back out into the corridor.

Meanwhile, Scott and Jack were on their way. They'd waited until the moment that the Saxon hordes first charged into view at the bottom of the hill – when all their fellow Cornish warriors were busy yelling war cries and brandishing weapons – before breaking rank and darting into the ruins. They met Emily and Drift in the huge grassy space in the centre of the castle. From the size of the room and the enormous derelict fireplace at one end, they guessed this had once been the great hall.

After a long search, the friends found the third pattern on one of the stones around the fireplace. There were hundreds of stones with similar patterns engraved on them but, by checking carefully against Scott's sequence, they were able to identify the stone that matched the pattern they'd found on the Carter toy box. It took a bit of jiggling, but at last Jack twisted it into place – just as they heard footsteps approaching.

The friends dived behind a pile of rubble and peeped

out to see two of the uniformed police officers who were helping the marshals with the History Week safety arrangements. 'I got a report of two boys in tunics and cloaks entering the castle . . .' one of them was saying. 'Kids up to some silly mischief, no doubt!'

'Actually, we're on a quest for the Holy Grail!' Jack muttered under his breath.

The officers had a quick look round and moved on.

The friends all breathed a sigh of relief. 'According to Lugg's clues, the next room is the lady's bedchamber,' Emily whispered. 'Where could that be?'

'I've been thinking about that,' Scott said. 'I bet it was directly above the great hall so that it would be kept warm by the heat from the big fireplace below.'

'Brilliant!' Emily said. But as soon as she looked up she realized they'd hit a major hurdle; all the floors above the hall had caved in long ago. There was nothing overhead but sky.

Scott pointed to the row of indentations – like empty tooth sockets – that extended along the stonework at about three metres above the ground. 'Those slots held the wooden beams that supported the ceiling and the next floor up.'

Emily took her binoculars from her bag and scanned the walls of what had once been the room above. There wasn't much to see, apart from gulls' nests and straggly weeds sprouting from the stonework. But then she spotted a row of carved stones along the bottom of a hole in the wall that might once have been a window. She gasped and handed the binoculars to Scott.

'That looks promising, but how are we going to reach them?' he said.

The words had hardly left Scott's mouth before Jack had shaken off his cloak and started to climb. He found a toehold, reached up and curled his fingers into a narrow gap and pulled himself up. It was no harder than the climbing wall at the sports centre, although he could have done with a few more colour-coded grips to cling to.

'Careful!' Scott yelled.

'Yeah, yeah,' Jack muttered. He was almost at the window now. He inched his foot onto a tiny ledge and eased upwards until his nose was level with the carved stones. Annoyingly, they *all* had those swirly line patterns on. How was he meant to know which was the right one? Hanging on with one hand, he tugged the rolled-up photocopy of Scott's pattern sequence from his belt with the other. He'd unfurled it with his teeth and was checking the patterns against the stones when he heard frenzied flapping and squawking.

'Watch out!' Emily cried.

It was too late. As Jack dodged away from the dive-bombing seagull he lost his grip. His heart tried to jump out through his mouth.

He was falling.

Without thinking, he grabbed his battle-axe from his

belt and swung it at the wall, wedging the blade into a crack like a mountaineer's ice-axe. It wasn't the strongest of holds. The blade was already slipping free, but it gave him just long enough to reach up with his free hand and grasp the stone with the pattern that looked the closest to the fourth in Scott's sequence.

To Jack's astonishment, the stone moved. He thrust it round a quarter turn before half tumbling, half scrambling back down the wall to land on top of Scott, who had positioned himself below, arms outstretched. They lay in a winded heap, Jack still clutching his battle-axe. Thinking it was a new game, Drift jumped on top of them, wagging his tail in delight.

'Quick! Get up!' Emily hissed. 'We've still got two more to find!'

'What about "Well done, Jack, for risking life and limb in a feat of awesome bravery"?' Jack grumbled.

'Yeah, that as well, but we haven't got much time. I just heard Mrs Loveday outside yelling, "Where's Emily with those carrots?"'

Jack grinned and leaped to his feet. 'Oh, no! We might be able to escape from the Saxon army, the police and the marshals, but if Mrs Loveday's on the warpath, we've got no chance!'

Scott sat up and brushed grass and flakes of stone off his cloak. 'According to Lugg's riddles, the next pattern should be in the toilet – where *a man comes out with less than he went in but still feels better.*'

Emily made a face. 'Where did they put toilets in castles?'

'Ooh, I know!' Jack said, hopping up and down as if he actually needed to make a visit. 'Follow me!' He sprinted out of the great hall, through an archway and into the tower that stood at the south-west corner of the ruins, closest to the cliff edge. Then he ran up the spiral staircase. Scott and Emily looked at each other, shrugged and ran after him, followed by Drift.

They found Jack kneeling on the third floor of the tower, examining the stones around a hole near the base of the wall.

'What are you looking at that little window for?' Scott asked.

Jack looked up at him. 'It's not a window. This is your top-of-the-range mediaeval en suite bathroom, or *garderobe*. There'd have been a wooden bench with a hole in it. The, er, waste products went out through here, down a stone chute, straight into the sea.' He paused and grinned. 'I remembered looking up from outside and seeing the chute jutting out from the wall last time we were here. Unlucky for any seabirds that happened to be swimming around down there.'

'How come you're suddenly an expert on Toilets Through the Ages?' Scott asked suspiciously.

Jack gave him a smug grin and tapped his nose. For once he'd actually remembered something from a school history trip! Usually, he was only interested

178

in the packed lunch and the riotous singing on the coach on the way home, but last year's outing to the Tower of London had been an exception: the details of the bathroom facilities in the White Tower had been revoltingly – and unforgettably – cool.

Meanwhile, Emily was kneeling, inspecting the stones beneath the chute. She found the pattern and, after a bit of digging with the blade of Scott's battle-axe to dislodge a thick layer of seagull droppings and moss, twisted it into position.

The three friends high-fived. 'Only one more pattern to go!' Scott laughed. 'The one in the tower.'

'Well, we're in one of the towers now,' Emily said, turning and running back to the stairs, tripping over the long skirts of her History Week costume in her haste. 'Let's go up to the top and try this one first.'

The boys and Drift followed. They came out on a wooden platform and stood for a moment, catching their breath after running up the steep spiral staircase. Looking over the turrets, they saw the glittering spectacle of the battle of Key Castle spread out below them. But there was no time to admire it. They were too busy inspecting every stone for a Celtic knot pattern.

There was no shelter from the scorching sun on the tower, and before long they were hot and thirsty and losing patience. 'This is hopeless,' Jack griped. 'Let's try one of the other towers.'

Emily was about to agree when she noticed Drift

snuffling at a pile of old sticks against one of the turrets. She pushed the sticks aside. Shading her eyes against the sunlight, she squinted at the wall behind. She could just make out the faint lines of a Celtic knot pattern.

The final piece of the puzzle!

This stone was much bigger than the other five had been.

Hardly able to breathe for excitement, Scott and Jack joined Emily and together they heaved the stone round in a clockwise half-turn.

Had they really solved the ancient secret of the Keepers of the Key?

Had they really found the hiding place of the Holy Grail?

Suddenly, with a clang of metal and a grinding of stone, a whole section of the turret slid to the side, to reveal a deep recess about the size of a microwave oven. The three friends knelt to look inside.

A ray of sunlight picked out a gleam of gold and a sparkle of red.

Jack couldn't wait a moment longer. He reached in and pulled out the object. It was made of metal and felt heavy and smooth and cool.

'Wow!' Scott whistled.

'We found it!' Emily breathed.

Even Drift yipped in surprise.

'I thought a grail was a kind of a cup,' Jack laughed, gazing down at the magnificent gold crown in his hands.

Each of its six points was set with a fiery red ruby, and a tall gold cross rose up in the middle. 'This is definitely not a cup!'

'That's because it's not the Holy Grail!' Scott said. 'I told you it wouldn't be.'

'A crown is way better than a *cup*! You can *wear* a crown, for a start. I wonder if it fits.' Jack was about to pop the crown on his head when he heard a noise on the stairs behind him.

He spun round. No doubt one of the History Week marshals had come to give them a massive telling-off for being off limits!

Never mind, Jack thought, gazing at the beautiful object in his hands. *It's worth getting a rocket to find this!*

He looked up, prepared for the worst.

At least he'd *thought* he was.

But now he was staring straight into those eyes again.

One black as night. The other milky white like the skin on a rice pudding.

Twenty-one

The New Keepers

'What?' Jack spluttered.

'But you're locked up in a cell!' Scott said.

The Hood took his time smoothing down his black robe. 'I escaped.'

'How?' Emily gasped.

The Hood's thin lips stretched into a chilling smile. 'I was being transferred from that one-horse police station to somewhere bigger. Truro, or Exeter, I believe.

Let's just say someone should have stowed his taser gun more securely in the police car. I seized the moment.' He gazed at the crown and smiled even more widely. 'So, I was wrong. The Keepers of the Key weren't guarding the Holy Grail, after all.' He laughed softly. 'I really should have guessed. It's the Crown of Avalon.'

'Did it belong to King Arthur?' Jack couldn't help asking.

'Oh, yes! Most people believe that the *Isle of Avalon* in the old writings refers to Glastonbury in Somerset. But, of course, I see it now. Avalon is Castle Key.' The Hood's sinister eyes were still locked on the crown. 'Whoever wears it will be the living embodiment of Arthur's spirit! I will have eternal life! *The king's power*!' He reached out, his knobbly fingers twitching with anticipation.

Jack hugged the crown closer to his chest. 'Oh, yeah, like we're just going to hand it over to you!'

The Hood leaned over so his face was close to Jack's. 'I have been a true seeker of the secret of eternal life for many years,' he spat. 'You kids merely stumbled upon it! *I* am the rightful owner!'

'But how did you find out about the Keepers of the Key?' Emily asked. She knew their only hope was to keep the man talking while they tried to come up with a plan to stop him getting the crown. She tried to catch Scott's eye, but he'd backed into a corner and huddled down into his cloak. *Surely he isn't going to give up without a fight?* she thought crossly.

The Hood sneered at Emily. 'In my years of studying the old manuscripts I had come across vague references to the legend of a secret society called the Keepers of the Key that was guarding an ancient relic of great power.' He pointed a finger at Jack. 'When I saw your question on the Arthurian Legends website about the Keepers of the Key story in Castle Key, I came to find out what the questioner – Mad Jack – knew about it.'

'Mad Jack?' Jack sputtered. 'That wasn't me!'

Scott looked up from his cloak. 'No, it was me. I sort of borrowed your name.'

'Cheers, mate!' Jack muttered.

The Hood took no notice. 'Of course, it was a stroke of luck that it was History Week here, so I could blend in by donning a monk's robe. And Lady Fortune smiled again when I met your friend, the old fisherman, and he directed me straight to you . . .'

'Yeah, so you started stalking us!' Jack snapped.

'And tried to kill us at the shepherd's hut,' Emily added.

'Only to *frighten* you into handing over the information that would lead me to my prize.' The Hood gazed at the crown again, like a Labrador drooling over a plate of sausages.

Jack could tell Emily was trying to keep the Hood talking. He hoped she was hatching a cunning escape plan because he certainly hadn't got one! All he could do was get on board with the keep-him-talking strategy and see where Emily was going with it. Trouble was, he was running out of polite conversation. 'Er, what happened to your eyes?'

The Hood touched his face. 'Many years ago I tried using alchemy to re-create the elixirs of eternal life described in ancient texts . . . I was dissolving gold in a blend of acids . . . There was an accident . . .' His voice tailed off as if he were suddenly tired of all this talk. 'Now hand me my crown!'

'*Your* crown?' Jack snorted. 'Finders keepers!'

Before Jack knew what was happening, the Hood snarled like a wild jackal and lunged for the crown. Scott and Emily tried to push him away, but the Hood snatched the crown out of Jack's grasp and shoved Emily aside. Scott tackled and knocked him off balance so that he staggered backwards.

As the Hood flailed his arms to break his fall, he let go of the crown. It soared into the air, the rubies flashing in the sun as it flipped over and over. Suddenly Drift leaped as if to catch a flying frisbee. He caught the crown in his teeth, but couldn't get a grip on the awkward shape. Instead, it flipped over his head like a hoopla ring at the fair. Drift cocked his head to one side. The crown slipped down over his ears and settled round his neck like an oversized collar.

He turned tail and ran.

The Hood tried to clamber to his feet and give chase

but Scott and Jack were too quick for him. They jumped onto his chest and pinned him down.

Meanwhile, Drift had reached the spiral staircase, where he narrowly avoided barrelling into a man on his way up: a tall man in Saxon breastplate and helmet, armed with a shield and a mighty sword.

It was only when he removed his helmet and they saw the thick black moustache that the friends recognized the Saxon warrior as Detective Inspector Hassan.

D. I. Hassan stood looking down at the Hood. 'Stewart Gibbs, you are under arrest. *Again!*'

Meanwhile, Drift trotted back up the stairs, still wearing the Crown of Avalon.

Emily knelt and hugged him.

'All hail, King Drift!' Jack laughed.

Scott gently removed the crown from Drift's neck and placed it back in the hiding place.

Emily looked up at D. I. Hassan. 'But how did you know where to find us?'

D. I. Hassan smiled. 'You should ask your friend here.'

Scott grinned. 'During that big charge at the start of the battle I noticed that one of the chiefs in the Saxon army was D. I. Hassan.'

'It's my day off,' D. I. Hassan pointed out.

'So, while Emily kept the Hood talking about Avalon and eternal life,' Scott said, 'I got my phone out under my cloak and sent a text to Carrickstowe Police Station asking them to call D. I. Hassan on his mobile and tell him he could find the escaped prisoner in the South Tower.'

'Genius!' Emily exclaimed.

'And I thought Em was the one with the plan! Good move!' Jack clapped his brother on the shoulder. 'I *might* just forgive you for the Mad Jack thing now!'

—

Two days later the Keepers of the Key held their first meeting since 1755 in the secret room at Stone Cottage. Lantern-light flickered over the faces of the small group gathered on the benches.

A silver-haired man in a pinstriped suit stood at the table in the middle. Roger Farnborough, the best lawyer in Castle Key, and a good friend of Old Bob, had been helping to draw up the legal agreement. He nodded at all present and held up a thick document. 'I have written up the details that you all agreed. The Keepers of the Key have reformed as a society of trustees, responsible for the safekeeping of the Castle Key crown.'

'You mean King Arthur's Crown of Avalon!' Jack chipped in.

The lawyer smiled at him. 'Which *some* believe to be the Crown of Avalon. But until that is proven, we will refer to it as the Castle Key Crown.' He cleared his throat. 'Now, where was I? Oh, yes. The trustees will include a representative of each of the six original families.' He smiled at Old Bob. 'First, Robert Trevithick.'

Old Bob, still sporting a bandage under his woollen cap, gave him a brief nod.

'Second, David White.' The lawyer looked across at Mr White, from Roshendra Farm, who responded with a tip of his tweed cap.

'Third, Matthew Goff,' the lawyer said.

The young man sitting next to Old Bob raised his hand. Goff had been easy to trace. He lived nearby in Carrickstowe and had carried on the family blacksmithing tradition by working as a farrier, making and fitting horseshoes.

'And Scott and I are the joint representatives of the Carter family,' Jack blurted.

Roger Farnborough nodded. 'Quite, quite! That's the Carter family taken care of. Unfortunately, we haven't been able to trace any surviving descendants of Josiah Lugg, so his place will be taken by the current curate of St Michael's church, Colin Warnock.'

Colin grinned and gave a thumbs-up. He'd swapped his brown monk's robes for his usual leather jacket, jeans and white collar.

The lawyer smiled again. 'Now for the final family, the Nancarrows. They've emigrated to Australia but I've spoken to them by phone. They asked for the society to elect someone to represent them here in Castle Key. Following a unanimous vote, this will be Miss Emily Wild, in recognition of the important part she played in rediscovering the crown.'

There was a round of applause.

Emily smiled shyly.

The lawyer looked back down at the document. 'So, to sum up, the Keepers of the Key all agree that the crown should remain in place at Key Castle and be looked after by the museum. Once the castle re-opens after the safety work is complete, the crown will be housed in a purpose-built display case in the tower so that it can be admired by the public – along with the Keepers of the Key scroll from 1755 and Josiah Lugg's notebook. Visitors will have a chance to try to work out the trail of patterns and clues to the hiding place for themselves, and there will be a plaque explaining the legend of the crown.'

Scott nodded in approval. He'd done a lot of research into the Crown of Avalon over the last two days. The old legends all seemed to agree that after being mortally wounded at the battle of Camlann, King Arthur had been taken to the Isle of Avalon. After that, things weren't so clear. There were many different theories as to where Avalon was, and what had happened to Arthur when he got there. Now there was a new theory to add to the list – Avalon was Castle Key, and Arthur had entrusted his crown to six ordinary Cornish men to guard throughout the ages . . .

'As trustees, you will meet once a year,' Roger Farnborough went on. 'You also agree to carry out regular inspections to ensure that the crown is safe.'

He licked his thumb and turned to the next page. 'And, following a special request from Jack Carter, we've added a clause to say that any Keeper of the Key is allowed to wear the crown at least once a year.'

Jack grinned at everyone.

'Membership of the society will be handed down within each family,' the lawyer continued.

'Yeah, but it won't just be to oldest sons,' Emily pointed out. 'It can be girls too. If they'd let girls in on the secret in the first place, it probably wouldn't have been lost when all those Keepers died in the tsunami in 1755.'

'Yes, we have added that, too,' the lawyer confirmed. 'Now, if you'd all like to sign . . .' He placed a pot of ink and an old-fashioned fountain pen on the old table and one by one the new Keepers stood up and signed their names on the document beneath the words:

The Keepers of the Key
We vow to uphold our pledge for the coming year

Emily was the last to sign. As she put down the pen she heard a commotion behind her. Drift and Boomerang came tearing down the steps into the secret room, playing chase. Boomerang sprang up onto the table and knocked the inkpot flying.

Emily whipped the precious document away just in time to stop the ink splashing all over it. But not before

Boomerang had run across the paper, adding a small black paw print to the agreement.

'Well, it *was* Boomerang who found the secret room in the first place!' Scott said.

'Yeah, great work, Boomerang!' Jack laughed.

'And you too, Drift,' Emily said, giving him a hug. 'We couldn't have solved Operation Key without you.'

The lawyer added a wax seal and rolled the document into a scroll, which he tied with a smart red ribbon. Then he handed it to Scott. Together with Jack and Emily, he carefully placed it inside the wooden chest and draped the gold cloth over to cover it up once more.

'Of course,' the lawyer said. 'We'll keep a copy in the safe at our offices too.'

'And on computer?' Scott suggested. 'This *is* the twenty-first century!'

'Now, who'd like a drink to celebrate?' Aunt Kate offered, coming down the stairs with a tray of champagne and sparkling elderflower cordial.

The Keepers of the Key all toasted each other.

Old Bob raised his glass. 'Until we all meet here again in a year's time!'

Emily, Jack and Scott clinked glasses. A whole year! Who knew how many more baffling mysteries they'd have solved by then?

Don't miss the next exciting mystery in the
Adventure Island series

THE MYSTERY
OF THE PHANTOM LIGHTS

Available August 2013!

Read on for a special preview
of the first chapter.

One

Night Fright!

Camping out on the moors was awesome, Jack Carter thought.

Until, that was, you woke up at two o'clock in the morning with an urgent need to go to the bathroom.

The moors were distinctly lacking in the bathroom department.

Which is why Jack was now stumbling around in the

dark searching for a conveniently placed gorse bush. A boy needed his privacy!

Mission accomplished, Jack stepped out from behind the bush and started back towards the tents, which were pitched on a flat patch of grass and heather halfway down a rocky slope. He picked his way over the rough ground. Although it had been a scorching August day, the night air was chilly. He shivered and sped up; his sleeping bag was calling to him.

That's when he slipped on a loose stone and fell flat on his face.

And that's when he realized he couldn't see the tents.

He must have strayed much farther from camp than he'd thought. In fact, he wasn't sure he was even heading in the right direction! He sat up and tried to get his bearings.

It was so dark that he could hardly make out the outline of the craggy ridge that rose up from the other side of the valley; it was just a smudge of blacker blackness against the black sky. And it was very quiet. *Too quiet!* Jack was a Londoner, used to streetlights and a soundtrack of car engines, sirens and snatches of music. Although he and his older brother, Scott, had been coming to stay with their great-aunt Kate for the holidays on the remote island of Castle Key for ages, while their dad was off on his archaeological digs, he still couldn't get used to all this nocturnal peace and quiet.

Jack stood up and looked back the way he'd come. Now

he could make out the outline of the tents in the distance, lit by the faint amber glow of nightlights through the canvas. He turned and hurried towards them.

Now he was on the right track again, he started hatching a plan.

Obviously, he was going to have to creep around outside the tent he was sharing with Scott and make some spooky noises. It would be a crime to miss this golden opportunity to give his brother a fright! Should he go for a ghostly wail, he wondered, or a snarling werewolf effect? The key thing was to make sure he got the right tent. (He'd learned that lesson the hard way on the school camping trip to Hatfield Forest, when he'd accidentally performed his entire mutant zombie scarecrow routine for his elderly geography teacher, Miss Bodley, instead of his mates, Josh and Ali. The shriek she'd produced when he lurched into her tent and shuffled round her sleeping bag had nearly burst his eardrums! There'd been letters home, detentions and grounding.)

But there was no danger of getting muddled this time; Jack and Scott's tent was a little apart from the rest of the group, next to the one that housed their friend, Emily Wild, and her faithful dog, Drift. And Emily's tent was hard to miss! It was more of a shelter than a tent, consisting only of sticks, leaves and a canvas sheet. And there was a rainwater catcher and a handcrafted washstand outside it. Emily liked to practise her survival skills whenever possible, in case she was suddenly called up by the security forces and sent off on a top-secret undercover mission in the wilderness. Scott and Jack had tried pointing out that, as she was only thirteen years old, this was unlikely to happen any time soon. But, as was so often the case, Emily didn't listen.

The remaining three tents belonged to other members of the Castle Key Nature Group. They'd all been taking part in a glow-worm survey. Nature had never really been Jack's thing, but earlier in the summer he and Scott and Emily had gone to see a pair of killer whales off North Point and, before they knew it, they'd been railroaded into joining the group. It had actually turned out to be very useful in solving the mysterious disappearance of an amazing supercar called the Black Salamander. Don Penrose, the group leader, had even awarded them their gold Nature Watch badges! It turned out that glow-worms weren't even real worms; they were beetles with luminous bums. It had been pretty cool, though, when they'd finally spotted the tiny green lights gleaming in the undergrowth.

Jack wasn't far from the tents and had just made up his mind to treat Scott to a bone-chilling werewolf howl when he heard a noise behind him.

A strange snuffling, shuffling noise.

He stopped in his tracks.

Maybe it was Scott or Emily trying to scare him. Or Drift out for a walk. But it couldn't be. Jack had kept his eyes fixed on the tents all the way back. He'd have noticed if anyone had come out.

There it was again! The noise was closer now. It sounded like the grinding of enormous teeth.

Jack's heart began to pound as if trying to break out of his ribcage with a sledgehammer.

Was it a *beast*? All these wild moor-type places had *beasts* prowling around ... A Bigfoot or a Yeti or a giant black panther with massive fangs like a sabre-toothed tiger ready to tear him limb from limb. He wanted to make a run for the tents but his legs seemed to think they were trapped in quicksand and were refusing to work. Jack closed his eyes and wished he were somewhere else – somewhere safe, somewhere with lights and shops and houses – somewhere like London ...

The beast was so close Jack could smell its meaty breath.

It was no good. He had to see what was about to eat him. Slowly, very slowly, he turned round.

His trembling torch beam picked out a pair of long, curved horns. Jack gulped. It wasn't just a beast, it was a *demon* beast! But then he saw the soft white ears, the big brown eyes, the long black and white face with the slightly dopey expression ...

Jack laughed out loud. He'd noticed the herd of goats earlier in the evening. They belonged to Roshendra Farm, and were let loose on the high moors to graze.

'Give me some warning next time you creep up on me, mate!' Jack said. 'I was that close to having to overpower you with my grip of death!'

The goat blinked and worked its jaws from side to side.

Jack patted the goat's neck and was turning to leave when he noticed three bright lights in the sky. White and red and green, they zoomed so low that they barely skimmed the ridge across the valley. They circled round and round, then hovered in one spot, shimmering and flashing, lighting up the shreds of cloud that floated in front of them with shades of blood red and ghostly green.

Below them, another light flickered on and off and darted about.

Jack stared at the lights. What were they? They were too bright and colourful for planets or stars, and you'd have to have a death wish to fly a plane that low over the ridge. But they were hovering too long to be fireworks. Could it be a helicopter? Surely he'd have heard the whirr of the rotors. And then there was the single light dancing beneath the others, almost as if it were calling to them.

Suddenly Jack knew what he was looking at: a UFO! An *Unidentified Flying Object* visiting Earth from a far-off planet! It was the only logical explanation. Just wait until Scott and Emily heard about this!

The lights seemed to be coming closer.

Uh-oh, Jack thought. He'd seen a programme on TV about alien abductions. Aliens beamed people up into their spaceships and experimented on them.

Jack didn't want to be an experiment.

'I don't know about you,' he whispered to the goat, 'but I'm out of here!'

But when he turned round, the goat had vanished!

THE ADVENTURE CONTINUES

Secret agent tests

•

Character profiles

•

Hidden codes

•

Exclusive blogs

•

Cool downloads

DO YOU HAVE WHAT IT TAKES?

Find out at
www.adventureislandbooks.com

the
orion star

Sign up for **the orion star**
newsletter to get inside information
about your favourite children's authors
as well as exclusive competitions and
early reading copy giveaways.

www.orionbooks.co.uk/newsletters

Follow @the_orionstar on .

Orion
Children's Books